# Shakuntala's Daughter



**Itirani Samanta**

Translated by
Dipty Patnaik

**Om Books International**

First published in 2024 by

**Om Books International**

**Corporate & Editorial Office**
A-12, Sector 64, Noida 201 301
Uttar Pradesh, India
Phone: +91 120 477 4100
Email: editorial@ombooks.com
Website: www.ombooksinternational.com

**Sales Office**
107, Ansari Road, Darya Ganj,
New Delhi 110 002, India
Phone: +91 11 4000 9000
Email: sales@ombooks.com
Website: www.ombooks.com



ISBN: 978-93-5376-976-5

Printed in India

10 9 8 7 6 5 4 3 2 1

Maa,

My life is exceptional in the sense that, unlike most children who have both their parents to help them stand on their feet, my father left us even before I could understand what the word meant. Single-handedly, you taught me to walk, struggle and march ahead despite adversity and obstacles. I learned to face up to life bravely even in extreme suffering. You opened up the world to me with your stories and idioms and, slowly but steadily, became my best friend. As I grew up, our relationship changed. In your way, you introduced the world to me while I experienced the same through my own perspective. I felt your presence within me and felt secure in you. By always being in my thoughts, you motivated the personality and behaviour of the characters I created in my works. Your stamp of approval was on everything I did.

You were with me when I started writing *Sakuntalara Jhia*. Little did I understand the strange irony of fate when you put your head on my lap and said goodbye. I could not believe it when you bade farewell with a simple phrase: "My girl, I am going." I screamed, shouted and cried but you did not respond. I became an orphan. The void left by your departure led to silence engulfing my life. Nevertheless, while I lost you physically, you are always at my side to guide and bless me. With this sincere debt of gratitude, I dedicate *Shakuntala's Daughter* to you and your memory.

Itina

# Preface

Women play major roles in my writing. I characterise them from my surroundings and various socio-economic strata. I pick up characters from the epics as well as history. Those who fascinate me leave a lasting impression, and I connect with their traits, personalities, and way of life. Their struggles and lifestyle invade my thought processes. I feel them in my heart, and then my brain embeds them in my thoughts. This constant churning in my mind creates the characters I write about, and Sakuntala is one of them. She refuses to concede defeat in the most fearsome of struggles for survival. She walks through life with courage and fulfils her determination to ensure a distinct identity for her daughter. She makes her daughter the harbinger of a new world.

*Sakuntalara Jhia* first appeared as a novelette in the October issue of *Kadambini*—the first-ever Odia monthly family magazine. The editing of *Kadambini* involved much of my time, and hence, recasting Shakuntala into a novel was delayed. With God's grace, it is now presented to you.

# Translator's Note

About four years or so back, I came across Dr Itirani Samanta's novella, *Shakuntalara Jhia*, in the magazine *Kadambini*, which she edits. I was deeply moved by its theme. Novels based around single mothers are rare in Indian literature. Behind the glitter of our society which preaches the values of morality, duty, family feeling, etc., there lurks a darker side where there is rampant sexual abuse and harassment, mostly by kith and kin. It's the worst-kept secret that belies the apparent societal harmony and the culture of compliance that permeate our existence. The pain increases a thousand-fold in a milicu of poverty and helplessness. The mother and child are shunned alike by society.

Dr Samanta's brave attempt to exhume the sufferings of a single mother by her kith and kin is commendable, and the very bravery of her venture compels me to translate the novel. Not surprisingly, at the first overture, I jumped into the project. Delays occasioned by the pandemic and a myriad of personal issues conspired to delay my efforts. Things came to a head, however, when I was recently accosted by the sight of a translation. A book can be translated several times with the author's permission, and my keenness remained undeterred. I felt that a fresh translation was in order, driven by my nuances, and to my joy, my fresh request found Dr Samanta's acceptance. I thank her profusely for her courtesy and, before embarking upon the attempt, do commend her daring to negotiate with a topic that even seasoned authors take a detour around.

I trust the readers will appreciate the narrative as much as I did.

# Chapter 1

Shakuntala gave the final touches to the food she had cooked. She was restless, for she was worried about the dinner being late.

If the elders were delayed, it would not matter much. However, the youngsters had to eat early, so she needed to finish the cooking in time.

She stirred the mixed vegetable curry. Okra had been fried, and she transferred it to a pot. She switched off the oven and reviewed what she had cooked. Unable to remember all the dishes, she uncovered the pots and checked them. She did not want to forget anything.

There were many people at home—Aunty's two sons, along with the elder one's wife, and daughter, along with her husband and children. A lot of food was needed. Everyone loved what she cooked. She knew the preferences of every family member and catered to them sincerely.

This family get-together at home took place a few times every year. The brother and sister who lived in other towns and their families got together with their parents whenever there was a short holiday. All of them, including the children, had a gala time. The house reverberated with the gaiety of the old and young. After a few days, they would go back, leaving behind Uncle and Aunty, plus the eldest son, Debu, and his wife, Kuni, and son, Liku.

Shakuntala stirred the mixed vegetable curry again. She wiped the gas stove clean and looked around the kitchen. Debu liked curd fish and small fish cooked in mustard gravy, while his brother and the children fancied country chicken cooked dry. The daughter and son-in-law preferred prawns cooked with coconut cream. For the vegetarians, she had prepared sweet and sour *moong dal*, with dry green mango pieces and gram flour pellets, stuffed *parwal* and okras, brinjals cooked in curd, fried spinach and cabbage curry. Shakuntala checked the pots again. She garnished the dishes with chopped coriander leaves and made a salad for the children.

Heaving a sigh of relief, she leaned against the wall and wiped her face with the loose end of her sari. She had been quite worried about finishing the cooking in time. Thank God, she had done it. She only had to sprinkle some cumin and chilli powder on the mixed vegetables and make the chapatis. She was not feeling well. Something was definitely wrong. At times, she felt like vomiting. God only knew what was wrong.

The family had been there for the past two days. She had not rested for even a moment, working tirelessly from morning until night. Aunty had left everything up to her, as always.

Shakuntala looked at the mixed vegetable curry once again. It was a favourite with Aunty. She had told her repeatedly the previous night, "Shakuntala! I leave the rest to you. But you must take special care to cook the mixed vegetable curry. My daughter loves it. The children get to eat different foods in their own homes but hardly the preparations we make. Who has the time to buy such a variety of vegetables and cook them properly? Who would soak green gram and chickpeas in water the night before so as to cook along with the vegetables? Who would take so much trouble? Such a variety of vegetables is also not available in cities. Let them eat something good when they are here. Besides, no one can cook mixed vegetables better than you. The aroma itself is enough to whet one's taste glands. Even I cannot cook it as well as you do."

Shakuntala sprinkled grated coconut and coriander leaves on the mixed vegetables. She also sprinkled a pinch each of cumin and chilli powder.

She wondered if she had added salt, feeling irritated with the uncertainty. However well cooked, a curry would be tasteless if it had no salt. She decided to ask someone to taste it—one of the sisters-in-law, perhaps. She went towards the living room and wanted to call either Aunty or Kuni Bhauja to taste the dish and tell her about the salt.

Shakuntala pushed aside the curtain of the living room, peeped through it, and saw that everyone was playing cards. She did not want to disturb them and so returned to the kitchen.

She was restless still. Someone had to taste the curry before she served it. What could she do? She could not taste it until at least one of the family members had eaten—it would be against protocol. Unable to overcome her anxiety, she finally picked up a spoon and sneaked a taste. Thank God! She had not forgotten the blessed salt. She washed her face and drank some water.

Suddenly, she developed severe pain in her abdomen. She had no idea what was happening to her as she had never felt such pain earlier. Its intensity was increasing.

She could bear it no longer as the pain began spreading all over her body. Her legs were wobbly. Oh no! She could not stand it any longer. She covered the dough, pressed her stomach with her hands, and sat down, thinking that would make her feel better. She drank some more water and then caressed her abdomen.

She was worried. There were still so many chores to be completed. She had to make the chapatis and feed the children. She had to serve the others too. She had to wash the utensils and clean up the kitchen. She wondered if the heat had affected her. She had been standing near the gas oven continuously for the past two days. Whenever Aunty's children came home, they had to be given appetising food. That was the least she could do for them. Besides, she loved cooking. She always monopolised the kitchen when guests arrived. No one else ventured inside.

Shakuntala drank some more water; it did not make her feel any better. The abdominal pain was increasing rapidly, and she was struggling to bear it much longer. She did not know what to do. The pain was too acute to be ignored. Shakuntala stood up slowly, supporting herself against the wall.

She closed the kitchen door and came out. Heading straight to the small room that was her bedroom, she rolled open a mat and lay down. She needed a little rest—just enough to be able to resume her duties somehow or the other. Work would come to a standstill if she lay down indefinitely. No one in the house even poured a glass of water for themselves. Everyone waited for her to serve them.

She looked at the clock and thought she could remain lying down for another ten minutes. But her abdomen was making her miserable—the pain kept growing. She could not put up with it anymore.

Shakuntala moaned and rolled on the floor.

"Shakuntala...! Where are you? The kitchen door is closed. Have you finished cooking?" She heard Aunty's voice but could not reply.

"Shakuntala...Hey, Shakuntala! Where are you?" Aunty called out again.

Shakuntala was in extreme agony. She could not reply even though she wanted to.

"What's wrong with you? Why aren't you answering? What are you doing in that dark room?"

Aunty entered and switched on the light. She asked, "Are you sleeping? Is something wrong?"

Shakuntala's face was bathed in sweat due to the excruciating pain. She groaned.

"Oh my God! What has happened? Why didn't you call me?" Aunty sat beside her and gave her a glass of water.

"Aunty! My stomach is hurting badly. I came here to lie down for a while. I thought I would get up when I felt better. I have finished cooking the dishes and was just about to make the chapatis. But the pain is unbearable. I can't take it anymore, Aunty!" It took her some effort to talk.

"I think you are in labour. What's this water everywhere? Don't you know anything? What else could be wrong with you? Your labour pains must have started! You don't have the foggiest idea about dates. How can anyone know? All right! Sleep here. Don't go anywhere. I'll get some help. It's already late at night. What am I going to do?" Aunty left the room worrying.

"Where is everyone? Debu dear! Please fetch Asha Didi from the next street. Kuni! Come quickly. The girl is in terrible pain."

Shakuntala was on the floor. Several thoughts ran through her mind. Aunty said that her labour pains had begun. Was she going to give birth to a baby? Was it really going to happen? Was she finally going to bring a child into this world? Was she going to hold it in her lap and breastfeed it? Was she really going to be a mother?

Shakuntala ran her palm over her abdomen. She thought that the baby had moved to the lowest part of her womb. It was repeatedly knocking on the door to come out.

"Oh God! The pain is intolerable."

"What's wrong, Shakuntala?" Kuni Bhauja asked. She sat beside her and caressed her forehead.

"The pain is insufferable. Oh God! Save me!" Shakuntala writhed in pain.

"You've got to be brave. Everything will be fine."

Asha Didi arrived, followed by Aunty.

"See, this is what's wrong! I think it's time. She might deliver any minute now."

"I think so. Why didn't you send for me earlier? I would have taken her in an autorickshaw to the nearby hospital. Does anyone deliver babies at home these days?" Asha Didi was aghast.

"I would have sent for you earlier had I known about it or if this girl had told me. She was busy cooking in the kitchen. I was in the living room along with the children. I got up a while ago to see what she was doing. And this is what I saw. Anyway, forget it. Examine her first. Don't waste time talking. Check how she is. God only knows since when she has been in labour. The stupid girl did not even have the sense to call me. The living room is full of people, and there is much noise there. I had no idea that something like this was happening. I came to know only when I found her here. I sent for you without wasting a moment."

"Aunty, the government provides incentive money when a woman delivers at a government hospital. She would have got some money. I too would have received some as an incentive. These days, I take everyone to the government hospital in the marketplace. I took two women there today. She has lost the chance of getting six thousand rupees; I too will lose," Asha Didi said while caressing Shakuntala's abdomen.

Shakuntala's pain was intensifying. She bit her lips hard and tried to put on a brave front.

"Who knows about all this? My son took my daughter-in-law to a nursing home when she was about to deliver. People talked about incentive money in our village. I never paid any attention to it. Besides, this girl does not remember the dates. I had no idea about the expected date of her delivery. Had I known, I would have made some arrangements. I had asked her several times, but she always said she didn't remember. The poor girl would have received some money at least. Anyway, there is no point in discussing it now. Please examine her. Help her deliver somehow. She has been in labour for a long time. I will get a glass of hot milk for her. Do something. You know what is to be done. I have been told that you are good at the work you do."

"Aunty, I work as an Asha *karmi* now. My job is not to deliver babies. We only take pregnant women to the hospital to get them checked."

"Don't tell me all that. You might be an Asha karmi now, but you have worked as a midwife earlier. You know what to do. You also know that we cannot get any other help at such an odd hour. Please help us out. Does anyone refuse to help at such a time? What would I do if you refuse to come to our aid? I will have to try to get someone else. I will have to find an autorickshaw to take her. Would any be available right now? I would have made some arrangements had I known about this earlier."

"All right. Don't worry. Let me see what I can do."

"I'll get some milk in the meantime." Aunty rushed out of the room.

"Make a cup of strong black tea. Add some dry ginger or black pepper if you have it. The delivery will be easy if she drinks it," Asha Didi instructed Kuni, who followed behind Aunty.

Asha Didi did her best. Shakuntala's agony was increasing. Several hours went by without anything happening. The pain receded at intervals, only to return with greater intensity. This was an acute state of labour.

The poor girl thrashed around and finally lay exhausted. She often screamed, rendering her throat parched. She pulled at her hair and hurt herself. Involuntarily, she scratched Asha Didi rather sharply, leaving bloody marks. Shakuntala bit her lips so hard that blood oozed out of them too.

"Everything is fine. The baby is in the right position. I fail to understand why it is not coming out. Why does the poor girl have to suffer like this? She would have delivered by now if we were in the hospital. At the most, a few stitches would be needed," Asha Didi said while caressing Shakuntala's head.

"The stupid girl didn't mention anything earlier. She was cooking throughout the day. I asked her several times if I could help. My daughter-in-law also asked her. Yet she did not allow anyone in the kitchen. She kept repeating that she could handle everything. I have no idea when the labour pains began. If only I had some inkling about it! No doctor will be available at any of the hospitals in the dead of night. Moreover, can we take her in an autorickshaw in her present state? Yet I have sent my elder son to get the autorickshaw." Aunty looked anxious.

"The driver must be drunk and sleeping. Even if he wakes up, one wonders if he can drive properly. Besides, the patient is in such a serious condition. Forget about him. Get another cup of black tea."

"I will get the tea." Kuni ran towards the kitchen again.

Shakuntala could not take it anymore. She invoked the presiding deity of her village and wailed, "Save me, Baba! Please save me. I cannot bear such pain any longer. Allow my child to be born safely. How much more suffering will you inflict on me? I have already gone through hell to bring this child into the world. Why are you playing such tricks with me at the final stage? How much more can I take?"

Shakuntala lay exhausted after her prayer.

The pain went on increasing. She was restless and too fatigued now to even thrash around. She felt as if someone was pulling her tongue out. There was darkness all around her. She cried out again, "O Lord! Why are you inflicting so much pain on me? Do what you want to do. I will take everything in my stride. But I have to tell you something. Give me as much pain as you wish and I will not complain. But no harm should come to my child. I will give birth to it. I am prepared to lay down my life for it. But I will not allow anyone to harm it in any way."

Asha Didi looked anxious. Aunty felt helpless.

"What's going to happen to her? Do something, Didi," said Aunty. "I have been praying for her. I don't know what else I can do." Her eyes moistened.

"Try again, my dear. Pray to the Lord for deliverance," Asha Didi told Shakuntala while stroking her abdomen.

Shakuntala was breathless because of the excruciating pain. It was extremely severe, something she had never experienced before. She recalled what her mother had told her: "It is not easy to be a mother. A woman goes through another birth in the process."

"Why do you say so, Bou? I cannot understand how a woman goes through another birth in the process of becoming a mother. A woman will give birth to a baby. How is she reborn?" Shakuntala had asked, bewildered by what she had been told.

"Why should it be difficult to understand? The baby comes out of the mother's womb by slicing her into two. Is it not the same thing as going through another birth? You will understand it when you deliver a little life. You will realise then how difficult it is to become a mother. Of course, she forgets all her sufferings when she sees the baby's radiant face."

Shakuntala now wondered when she was going to forget her suffering. Why wasn't the baby coming out? It was becoming more and more unendurable every minute. Would she be able to bear the pain much longer? She thought she would not live through the ordeal. She was losing all hope of ever looking at her baby's face.

All of a sudden, another agonising wave of pain ran through her abdomen. Shakuntala screamed aloud and passed out.

The baby finally came into the world.

Asha Didi cut the umbilical cord and separated the child from its mother.

There was deadly silence. The baby did not make any sound. Aunty sprinkled water on Shakuntala's face to revive her. Asha Didi cleaned the baby and shook it to make it cry. She pinched its buttocks. It did not work. Shakuntala remained inert. The baby too was quiet, its eyes closed.

Everyone was worried. Why wasn't the baby crying? What was wrong with it? Asha Didi placed her hand several times in front of the baby's nose to see if it was breathing; it was. She had no idea what else she could do. She covered it and looked at Aunty.

Asha Didi's voice shook as she said, "This is beyond me, Aunty. I don't know what more we can do. The baby was born under such difficult conditions. Why doesn't it cry?"

"Examine it more carefully. What could be wrong?" Aunty asked as her eyes welled up.

She continued, "Oh Asha! What should we do now? I am confused. What could have gone wrong with the mother and the baby? The child was born after so much trouble. And look at it now! Where can we take them both so late at night? Where will we find a doctor? What to do? My children will blame me for not taking Shakuntala to the hospital in time. How can I explain it to them? No one will forgive me if something happens to the mother or the baby." Aunty sobbed.

"Be patient. Asha Didi is trying her best. Everything will be fine," said Kuni, placing a hand on Aunty's shoulder.

"What's the matter with the poor girl? And I dare not think of what is going to happen when she regains consciousness and finds her child like this! She went through all kinds of trouble just to bring it into this world. She wanted to be addressed as 'mother'. Everything has come undone now. The stupid girl never informed me about her dates. We could have taken her to a doctor in advance if we knew. I tried several times to take her for a check-up but she refused to go.

"She had said, 'The doctor will ask me too many questions and I won't be able to answer them. Don't worry on my account, Aunty. The presiding deity of my village will set everything right. I am not going to spare Him otherwise.' What could I have done in such circumstances? Why has God played such a game with the unfortunate girl? The child should have been born healthy. She would have spent her days happily with it. What will happen now? What will happen to Shakuntala when she recovers? How am I going to explain it to her? Please examine the baby once again. See if you can do something. The people in this house will make my life miserable. My elder son is fuming in the other room. He had gone to call Dhadia, the auto driver, but he was not at home. Manua, who rents out his autorickshaw, told my son on the phone that he would tell him about the driver's whereabouts soon. What else could I have done?" Aunty wept, unable to continue talking.

"How can you be held responsible? Why do you think that people will blame you for all that has gone wrong? You have done everything that you could do." Aunty's daughter came and stood beside her.

"Don't worry. Everything will be fine. Shakuntala has suffered a great deal. Therefore, she has become unconscious. The baby is fine. The only problem is that it's not crying. It might cry any time now. Don't worry. We cannot do anything more. God will set everything right. Your blood pressure will rise if you get worked up like this," Mituna consoled her mother.

"Why isn't Shakuntala regaining consciousness? Asha has sprinkled water on her face several times already," Aunty said in response.

Asha Didi took the baby and placed it beside Shakuntala. She slapped it hard and pinched it also. The wee thing finally broke its silence with a loud wail.

Everyone around broke into relieved chatter and Shakuntala opened her eyes.

Aunty exclaimed, "Did you see how the mother recovered as soon as the baby cried? Everything is indeed in God's hands. This mother-child duo is making us dance to its tune. I was almost going out of my mind worrying."

Asha Didi addressed Shakuntala. "Look here. See who is sleeping beside you. The two of you have given us a lot of trouble."

Aunty added, "Sit up, Shakuntala. Look! What a cuddly little girl you have! Her face is a replica of yours—she even has thick, curly hair like you. Here, take her in your lap." She held up the baby to Shakuntala.

The new mother had to make an effort to sit up. Aunty placed the baby in her lap. Shakuntala clasped her daughter to her chest while tears rolled down her cheeks.

Asha Didi said, "Don't press the baby to your bosom so hard. She will suffocate. Besides, what is the point of clutching her so? Give her what she needs. How she is crying for it! It would seem the world will come crashing down. Place your nipple into her mouth quickly. Her throat must be parched. Such a long time has already passed."

Shakuntala was completely exhausted. She did not think she had the strength in her arms to hold the baby. The little one might slip out of her trembling hands, she worried. But she collected herself the next moment and said, "It is not good for me to act like this. How can I go through life if I am so weak? I have to get on and be firm. I have to do much for my daughter."

She held the baby close to her chest and covered her with the end of her sari. She seemed enchanted and contented. Her fatigue seemed to have evaporated. She kept caressing her daughter and quietly paid her respects to the presiding deity of her village.

"I'll go now, Aunty. It's quite late." Asha Didi made a movement to leave.

"Why don't you eat something here before you go? The girl had cooked such a great lot today. No one ate peacefully tonight. Everyone only pecked at the food. A lot of it is left. Wash yourself. I will ask Kuni to serve you. Eat something before you go."

"No, Aunty. I will go home and bathe. I don't feel like eating anything right now. I will just have a cup of tea and go to bed. I cannot eat anything so late at night." Asha Didi was in a hurry to leave.

Shakuntala lifted a corner of her mattress and took out a small purse. She would receive a few rupees in tips whenever Aunty's children came home. She had saved it all. She did not have to spend on anything as Aunty took care of all her needs. What did she need money for?

"Didi, you have pulled me out of the jaws of death. My daughter and I would have been in bad shape if you had not come in time. I cannot thank you enough. What else can I give you? Take this, please." She took out a hundred-rupee note from the purse.

"Why are you giving her money? Won't I pay her? Keep your money with yourself," said Aunty.

Asha Didi snatched the money eagerly and put it inside her blouse. She said, "Let her give the money, Aunty. She has given birth to her daughter after so much suffering. Let her give something happily. Besides, this amount is nothing. You can pay me separately. This is something that she has given me out of happiness. You will pay me for my labour."

"Since you will take money from me, why are you taking from her? How much money does she have with her after all?"

"Let me tell you something, Shakuntala. Because of Aunty, I am leaving with whatever you have given me. But you still have to give me sweets and a sari! Big *laddus* made of pure ghee and a red sari with a wide border. Don't forget!"

Aunty said, "Oh, come on, Didi! Do you think the poor girl can afford to give you these presents? She fills her own stomach somehow by working in someone else's house. Now she has a child to feed too."

"You will give me my fair share. But she too has to give me something. She has given birth to a daughter. Goddess Laxmi has blessed her."

"All right! Off you go!"

"Don't listen to Aunty, Shakuntala. Remember what I said. Don't you forget it!" Asha Didi laughed and left soon after.

Shakuntala sat covering her daughter with her sari. The child had already dozed off with the mother's nipple in her mouth. She too was exhausted. After all, she too had undergone a great deal to come into the world once again.

Aunty returned with a bundle of old clothes and kept it beside Shakuntala. "Take these. Tear them into small pieces and use them for the bleeding. I will tell Kuni to give you her son's old clothes for the baby."

"Those will come later. Drink this first, Shakuntala," said Kuni, placing a bowl of sago porridge beside her.

"I cannot eat or drink anything now. I feel nauseous. I will drink it after a while. Go and sleep. It's late and you are awake for my sake. I am so embarrassed. Please go and sleep."

"Drink this first without talking so much. You have suffered a great deal. I would have certainly died if I had suffered like you."

"Oh! Why do you say such inauspicious words?" Shakuntala recalled the time when Kuni had delivered her child.

She knew that Kuni had been a pampered child, whose tolerance for pain remained low even in adulthood. The expected date of delivery was still fifteen days away when she felt mild discomfort in her abdomen. Debu took leave from work and took everyone in a car to Cuttack. Shakuntala too had gone with them. Since that day, Kuni stayed in a nursing home until the birth. During that time, both the families arrived there. Kuni's mother sat by her side, looking after her every minute of the day. Aunty gave her milk and Horlicks at regular intervals. Several doctors examined her repeatedly. She was wheeled into the operating theatre the moment she went into labour. Everyone was euphoric when told that a son had been born.

The family conveyed the good news to others. Uncle and Kuni's father immediately bought large laddus and distributed them in the nursing home. Kuni stayed there for ten more days before returning to the village hale and hearty.

When the villagers came to see her, everyone was given sweets. There was a festive atmosphere at home for twenty-one days. A *satyanarayana* puja was held on the twenty-first day in the company of friends and relations. A sumptuous feast was arranged for everyone in the village. The celebrations were done with pomp and ceremony. Kuni then left for her parents' home. Uncle and Aunty happily sent her off to rest there. Of course, no one would have given her any work if she had stayed back with her in-laws. Shakuntala was there. She would never have allowed Kuni to do anything. The new mother stayed at her parents' place for three months.

Shakuntala did all the housework and tended to her newborn child also. When Kuni returned, she did not have to do anything.

"What are you thinking, Shakuntala? Drink the porridge. Your daughter is sleeping because her stomach is full. She will get up in a while and bawl for food. How will you have any strength to feed her if you do not eat? You have to drink this whether you like it or not or whether it tastes good or not. You just have to drink it. You have to think of her welfare in whatever you do. Come on! Drink this quickly. I will leave only after you drink it," Kuni said affectionately.

Shakuntala drank the porridge without any further fuss.

"Sleep now. We will take care of the rest in the morning."

Aunty and Kuni closed the door behind them.

Shakuntala was drained. She felt as if there was no life in her limbs. Her eyelids drooped. She thought she could sleep uninterrupted for two full days if she allowed herself to doze off now. But she just could not. She was scared that she might not wake up when her daughter cried for milk. The baby was just a day old. Her throat would become parched if she cried for long. Shakuntala could not allow that to happen. No, she would sit with the baby in her lap. It would be tough for her, but she was willing to make the sacrifice.

# Chapter 2

Shakuntala was a mother now.

A considerable change had come in her life that had altered her lifestyle too. Everything changed after the birth of her daughter. She now had a reason to live and she did so with renewed vigour.

She paid little attention to her physical and mental distress. Could she sit still just because she was not perfectly fit? Earlier, there was only one stomach to fill; now, there were two. The baby needed milk as well as medicines. How would she make ends meet if she just sat with the baby in her lap all day? She forced herself to return to work and soon took over the responsibility of Aunty's household as before.

"Hey, Shakuntala! What name have you chosen for your daughter?" Aunty asked Shakuntala one day.

"How can I choose a name for her? She has come into this world by your grace. All this happened because God placed me in your care. Neither my daughter nor I would have survived otherwise. No one can say what would have happened to us. You name her. She needs your blessings to survive in the world," Shakuntala replied as she fed her daughter.

"All right! All right! Take a bath and do wash your hair. Bathe your daughter too in warm water. Take her to the Shiv temple in the village and perform puja for her there. She has completed one month today. Do you remember it or not?"

Shakuntala had forgotten that her daughter was now one month old.

Aunty continued, "Take care! Don't bathe for a long time. Be careful about your daughter too. She might catch a cold. You are already doing all the chores at home. Thankfully, you and your daughter are healthy. You are lucky that way. Anyway, go and bathe. Oh, yes! Kuni has new clothes for the baby and a new sari for you. Both of you dress in them. We want to see how you look."

Shakuntala gave her daughter a warm bath and put the new dress on her. She put a large black mark on her forehead to ward off evil spirits, carried her to the prayer room and paid obeisance to the deities. Finally, she went to Uncle and Aunty to pay her respects before heading towards the temple.

Uncle put a five-hundred-rupee note in the baby's hand.

Shakuntala asked, "Aunty, have you thought of a name for my daughter?"

"Yes. Uncle has chosen a good one."

Shakuntala looked at Uncle expectantly.

"Tell it to her. How eagerly she is waiting to hear it!" Aunty said with a laugh.

Uncle responded, "I have been thinking about it since the day she was born. Finally, I have decided on one that I really like. Name your daughter Bharati. This is another name for Goddess Saraswati. I hope your daughter will study a lot and become someone important one day. She will make her mother forget all her sorrows."

Aunty sweetly said, "Her golden girl will surely do so. A daughter has entered Shakuntala's life. She will live happily from now onwards."

Shakuntala was indeed happy and contented. Clasping her daughter to her chest, she paid her respects to the old couple once again.

"Bless my daughter, please," she said.

"We bless her with all our hearts. Go to the temple now and tell the priest to perform a puja for her. Take this ten-rupee note from me and give it to the priest as his honorarium." Aunty handed over the money.

Shakuntala covered her head with the end of her sari and her daughter with a corner of it and left for the temple.

Day by day, the infant grew healthier. Several other things changed in the process too.

# Chapter 3

Shakuntala was cooking when she heard her daughter crying and rushed to her. The girl was lying flat on her belly on the bed. Shakuntala was amazed and ran straight to Aunty, exclaiming, "Look, my daughter has turned over by herself!"

"This is nothing. She will perform several miracles in future. Just be patient."

Many a time after that, Shakuntala found the child on her belly. At times, the child would accidentally bang her face on the floor. She would cry loudly and quiet down only when her mother cradled her in her arms.

On one occasion, Shakuntala deliberately ignored the child. She wanted the girl to get used to being alone. She had made her mind up to do the household work diligently in spite of the additional responsibilities of a mother. No one should develop negative feelings for the child and think that she was rendering her mother neglectful of work, resolved Shakuntala. It would bring bad luck to the baby. Besides, earlier, Aunty had only one person to provide for. Now there were two. Aunty also had to buy medicines and injections for the baby. How much could the young woman expect her employers to do for her?

Shakuntala tried to save some of Aunty's expenses. Instead of expensive allopathic medicines, she took recourse to homeopathy for her daughter's minor ailments. The medicines came cheap, and she bought them with her own money.

To ensure that no one complained about sloppy work, Shakuntala worked with increased dedication and devotion. She often left her daughter by herself while working. She began work early and finished late. It was then that she smothered the child with love and a lot of baby talk. Thinking that she had not fed the child adequately in the day because of work, she fed her several times during the night.

# Chapter 4

While playing with her daughter one night, Shakuntala heard a special word ringing in her ears: "Ma." She was astonished and seemed transported to another world. She picked up her daughter, kissed her frantically and excitedly said, "Say that again! Say that again!"

"Ma!"

"Say it again!"

"Ma! Ma!"

Shakuntala's joy knew no bounds. The fulfilment she experienced was unbelievable. Bharati's repeated utterances of "Ma" reverberated through her.

Soon, the little girl was wobbling around. She was sleeping less now, and Shakuntala found it difficult to spare time to teach her child to walk. Bharati often tried to stand up by clinging to a wall or a chair. After a while, she could take a few shaky steps without any support. Though she often fell soon after, announcing her defeat with loud cries. Shakuntala was, however, amazed to see Bharati's determination; even after falling several times a day, she would go on trying to walk.

Aunty looked after the two children—Kuni's son, Liku, and Shakuntala's Bharati. However, it was a difficult job. Liku was about seven to eight months older than Bharati and would not sit still. He ran around wildly and tossed things at people. He hardly slept during the day and kept everybody on their toes. Even his father had to constantly chase after him in the evenings to keep track of his son. Liku ran to Bharati at the slightest pretext. He would hold her hand, drag her by the arm and push her down. He beat everyone in the house, including Bharati, with anything he could lay his hands on.

Surprisingly, Bharati rather liked Liku. At times, she looked at him thoughtfully before breaking into a smile and running after him.

Shakuntala enjoyed seeing the children together. However, she was apprehensive that Liku might unintentionally hurt Bharati. The little boy usually woke up late. Kuni woke him up only after her husband had left for office. Shakuntala, however, ensured that Bharati was up early. She kept her awake till late at night and deliberately woke her up early in the morning. Bathed and fed, the girl would sleep through most of the day. This routine was in keeping with her mother's work timings. Shakuntala also believed it was better for Bharati to sleep when Liku was on the rampage. They were not likely to quarrel then. She tried her best to keep them apart. Thus, Liku and Bharati hardly met each other during the day. Besides, this way, Bharati was well rested in the evenings and could play with her mother when she got off work. At times, Shakuntala wished that God had given her four hands instead of two.

Once, Uncle, Aunty and Kuni went to the temple with Liku. They had been invited by Henna Aunty to a family function in the village.

Shakuntala did not have much work that day. She finished cooking and went to her room, where Bharati was sleeping peacefully. While folding and putting away the freshly laundered clothes, she glanced at Bharati from time to time. She realised that Aunty was right when she had said that her daughter's face looked exactly like her own. The round mark that she put on Bharati's forehead every morning was now smudged. Shakuntala wiped it clean and made another. Bharati had become quite naughty of late. She would struggle when Shakuntala put the mark. The young woman used force to succeed but often failed when she tried to apply kajal on her daughter's eyelids. Thank God Bharati was turning out to be a beautiful girl. Shakuntala was happy and content. She breastfed her regularly and occasionally gave her porridge made of *chura* powder, i.e., a paste of rice and lentil. Her own milk was the major source of nourishment for Bharati, while Liku survived mainly on tinned milk powder. Aunty had often said that she would get milk powder for Bharati too. However, Shakuntala refused.

Shakuntala was elated seeing her daughter grow. The girl was quite well built, though not overweight. She was extremely fair and had hair on her head since birth. It had grown strong and thick. Shakuntala had not shaved the child's scalp yet but planned to take her to the Shiv temple one day soon for her *mundan*.

Shakuntala played with Bharati in the afternoons on days when she was free. At times, she tied her hair in a beautiful knot. Bharati preferred boys' clothes because only one or two frocks had been bought for her. Most of the time, she wore Liku's hand-me-downs. Therefore, it was only to be expected that she would often wear male attire.

Shakuntala finished putting away all the clothes. She was grateful that Liku had been born some months before Bharati. They might be boys' clothes but Kuni had given her so many of them that Bharati had enough to wear. Shakuntala could not have bought these many clothes on her own. She made obeisance to the presiding deity of her village for them.

Shakuntala lifted Bharati's palms and brushed them against her own cheeks. She bent down to kiss her but promptly straightened up when she remembered that Aunty had once chastised Kuni for showering love on a sleeping child. She continued to stare at Bharati who was growing more and more beautiful with each passing day. And then she cursed herself for risking jinxing her daughter with her unchecked adoration. She spat on her daughter to offset any ill effects and recalled her mother saying that it boded ill for a child if its mother took too much pride in its good qualities.

A flicker of a smile crossed Bharati's face.

Shakuntala too smiled. She was sure that Goddess Sathi, the goddess of children, was making her smile. Her grandmother had told her in her childhood that the goddess loved children and appeared in their dreams singing lullabies. Her sweet voice made them smile while they slept soundly.

Bharati turned on her side. Shakuntala wondered whether she should wake her up as she was free at the moment. The house seemed so lonely when no one was around and she had no idea when the family would return.

Looking intently at the child, Shakuntala suddenly remembered something.

She had soaked rice and black gram. Rushing to the kitchen, she started grinding the mixture vigorously.

# Chapter 5

The days passed by. Bharati was growing up and would soon be a big girl, old enough to go to school. Shakuntala wondered what she would do. She knew that Uncle and Aunty would feed and clothe the mother and daughter but would they pay for Bharati's schooling? How could she ask them to do that? Was her daughter going to sit at home without studying?

The lady from the neighbouring house was talking to Aunty the other day. She had said, "How many people are you going to feed at home during such hard times? How long do you think this can go on? You kept this girl at a time when Kuni was pregnant and you needed someone to help you. That work is done now. This girl is no longer alone either; she has a growing child. Send them away while there is still time. You may find it difficult to do so after a while."

"Let me see what I can do," Aunty had said haltingly.

"What do you mean by that? Do you have any idea what your children will tell you later?"

"Let us see. Everything depends on God's will."

"Forget God's will; you have to decide. Your daughter-in-law doesn't say anything for now. However, when Shakuntala's daughter grows up and quarrels with Kuni's son, will she keep quiet? The interests of her child come first for any mother.

Everything was fine as long as there was no other child at home. The situation has changed. How can Shakuntala's daughter and your grandson live under the same roof? Will you treat Bharati in the same way as you treat Liku?"

"I admit you have my best interests at heart. I have to think. People will say that we kept her when we needed her and drove her away when she needed it. That is not good. Let me think about it. I will decide soon."

The neighbour would have perhaps gone on and on, but she saw Shakuntala and became quiet. Shakuntala's heart was heavy after what she had heard. She was more worried than before.

The neighbour was not completely wrong. Two children of the same family can and do live under one roof. But Liku and Bharati were not equals. There was a world of difference between them. Liku was born into a rich family and was a pampered child. There could be no comparison between the two. Shakuntala understood it but what could she do? Where could she go? Her mind was fixed on her predicament. Whom could she ask for help?

Aunty came into the kitchen in a panic and shook her out of her reverie. "What are you doing here? How can you be so absent-minded? Can't you hear your daughter crying so loudly?" Aunty switched off the grinder and virtually dragged her out of the kitchen.

Shakuntala heard Bharati bawling so loudly that it sent shivers up her spine. Her head was spinning.

Kuni had Bharati in her lap. The child was bleeding profusely from her head and the blood had spread all over her face. Liku was standing beside his mother.

Shakuntala did not know what to do. She started crying. When did this happen? Was she so lost in her thoughts that she did not hear Bharati crying? Her mind stopped functioning as she stood rooted to the spot. Her strength sapped and her feet were heavy. Bharati kept crying and stretched out her hands towards Shakuntala. Kuni carried the girl to her and said, "Shakuntala, take your daughter in your lap." Shakuntala pressed Bharati to her bosom. She wiped the blood from her face with a corner of her sari but the little girl pushed her hand away. Blood continued to flow. Shakuntala's sari was stained scarlet at the edges.

Aunty brought a handful of sugar and pressed it to the wound but Bharati continued to bleed. She was semi-conscious now.

Holding her child, Shakuntala ran down the village street.

"Shakuntala! Where are you going? What happened to your daughter? Why is she bleeding?"

"Did she fall down? Oh my God! She is bleeding badly."

"Where are you taking her?"

"She must be taking her daughter to the primary health centre in the neighbouring village. Will the doctor be available there at such an odd hour?"

"The doctor comes from the city once in two to three days and sits for an hour or two at the most. He won't be there now."

"Shakuntala! Be careful! The child will be hurt if you stumble and fall! It is already in a bad state."

People on the street saw Shakuntala running blindly and made many a remark. Shakuntala did not hear anything. She just kept running, oblivious to the surroundings and the comments.

She reached the health centre in the neighbouring village just as the nurse was leaving.

"Didi! Please examine my child." Shakuntala almost collapsed with Bharati in her arms. The child had lost consciousness.

"This is a serious case. The doctor has left. I can't handle it on my own," the nurse said. Bharati stirred and began crying again when the nurse touched her. She was resisting any attempt at being handled.

"Do something, Didi. My child is in severe pain. Stop the bleeding at least. It seems that all the blood she has will flow out," Shakuntala pleaded and fell to the nurse's feet.

"Be quiet for a while! The doctor would not have gone very far. I'll ring him up."

After speaking to him, she reassured Shakuntala, saying, "Don't worry. He had not gone very far. He is returning and will examine your daughter."

She continued, "Bring the child here and place her on the bed. Hey, Shankar! Come quickly."

However, Bharati clung to Shakuntala and would not lie down. She put her arms tightly around her mother and kept crying. Even when the doctor arrived and tried to examine her, she would not leave Shakuntala.

The nurse finally managed to make Bharati lie down. The gash was stitched and a few injections given. The doctor prescribed some medicines and more injections while the nurse explained how they were to be administered. Meanwhile, Bharati began to doze off. Shakuntala expressed her gratitude to all the gods and goddesses and thanked the doctor and nurse for their timely help. She hoped that the pain would subside once Bharati fell asleep.

Aunty and Kuni were sitting in the living room when Shakuntala and Bharati returned. Aunty asked, "How is your daughter? I tried to follow you to the hospital but Liku was so frightened that he clutched my sari and would not let me go. Was the doctor there?"

"He had left but the nurse called him back. He has stitched and bandaged the wound and given some injections. He has also prescribed medicines and injections."

"All right. Lay the child on the bed and let her sleep for a while. Come and eat something."

Kuni said apologetically, "I am really sorry, Shakuntala. The postman was at the door when we returned from the temple. We spoke to him for a moment while Liku ran into the house. I knew that you were inside but did not know when he ran to Bharati and hit her on the head. The poor child is suffering only because of our negligence."

"What had to happen has happened. Don't think about it now. Liku too is only a child. Does he know what he has done? All this has happened because of me. I was working with the grinder and was completely lost in thought. I had no idea that my daughter had come out in the courtyard. I didn't even realise that all of you had returned. Neither did I hear Liku."

Aunty said, "All right! It's over now. Bharati is sleeping. Come and eat something. She will cry as soon as she gets up. She won't let you out of her sight. The pain will return then. The poor girl has had to suffer a lot today."

Shakuntala had lost her appetite. She felt that the blood that had flowed from Bharati's wound had flowed out of her too. Her poor child was in so much pain. How could she eat at such a time? Her daughter hadn't eaten anything since yesterday.

"Why don't you come and eat?" Aunty said again. Thinking that Aunty and Kuni would feel bad if she did not eat, she put Bharati on the bed slowly and forced herself to swallow a morsel or two. Her limbs were lifeless and later, she went about her chores mechanically.

Bharati was still asleep when Shakuntala went back to her room after finishing her work. She sat beside her and was startled when she discovered that Bharati was running a high fever. Lines of worry etched her forehead. As the child's head was bandaged, she could not sponge her burning forehead. She fanned her after wiping her body with the corner of her sari.

Aunty rang up the doctor, who then prescribed some additional medicines for Bharati. She sent for them. Shakuntala spent the whole night with Bharati in her lap. The child would wake up often and cry. Shakuntala tried to feed Bharati but could not. In the morning, the fever had somewhat subsided but Bharati stuck to her lap and refused to lie down. Shakuntala also did not want to leave her daughter alone.

The fever rose again by the afternoon. Bharati was almost unconscious most of the time and did not drink even a drop of water. Shakuntala invoked the presiding deity of her village, praying, "O Lord! Punish me in any way but spare my daughter, please."

The fever went on rising slowly and Aunty forced her to take Bharati to the government hospital near the marketplace. Shakuntala felt bad that Aunty was spending more money on Bharati but she did not have any other choice but to accept.

The child had to stay in the hospital for a week. Aunty insisted that Shakuntala remain there with Bharati until she had fully recovered. When they both returned, Shakuntala felt rather guilty at having stayed away so long and set to work immediately. She did not allow Kuni to help and told her to look after Liku. "You have nothing to do here as I am now back. I am embarrassed I had to stay in the hospital for such a long time and you had to do all the work and also take care of your child. You must have gone through a lot of trouble."

# Chapter 6

One day, Shakuntala was washing the utensils in the backyard when she told Aunty, "If you have picked the flowers, shall I make some tea for you?"

"Not now. Maybe after some time. Finish what you are doing."

"Let me make a cup of tea for you first. Has Uncle got up?"

"He is still sleeping. We will have tea together when he gets up. Wash your hands and come with me for a minute."

"Where?"

"Come with me. I have to tell you something."

"What is it?"

"Come with me first."

Shakuntala followed Aunty across the backyard to the neighbouring house.

She thought Aunty probably wanted it cleaned. It belonged to a distantly related brother-in-law.

Shakuntala had noticed that it was always locked but the key was with Aunty who would engage a few labourers every now and then to get it cleaned. Her brother-in-law had died long ago and his three sons did not seem interested in the house. They rarely visited the village and had therefore left the key with Aunty.

Shakuntala recalled that the sons had come once during the puja vacation and had stayed in the house for two days. While leaving, they had said, "Aunty, please get the house cleaned at regular intervals, otherwise white ants will destroy everything. We cannot come here very often. The house is in your charge now and you please do your best. We have already sold all our land except this home, with which our memories are associated. No one wants to come here and we do not want to dispose of it. We remember how Papa had struggled to build it. All of us spent our childhood here and we can never sell it. As long as we are alive, we will come occasionally, and after that our children can decide what to do."

Aunty was now recounting this to Shakuntala, who wondered about the reason behind the narration. She had never been instructed to clean that house. What did Aunty want to tell her here that she could not have said at home? Shakuntala was apprehensive as these questions raced through her mind.

Aunty entered the house through the back door and stood in the courtyard. Shakuntala followed her and looked at her questioningly.

Halting between words, Aunty said, "I want to tell you something, Shakuntala. But don't misunderstand me." She paused.

A few moments later, she continued, "I think you and your daughter should live here. It is vacant all the time. Those people come once every two or three years. It is deteriorating because no one lives here. My getting the house cleaned once in a while does not help."

Shakuntala kept staring at Aunty. The earth seemed to be slipping from under her feet. She was in a dilemma. Had she done something wrong? Did Aunty have a change of heart? Was she worried about the large sums she had spent on

Bharati? Shakuntala was alone earlier; now there were two. The neighbour was probably right when she had asked with concern how much of a burden Aunty could take upon herself to care for them both.

Where could she go if Aunty drove her out? What would she do? Besides, she now had a daughter. Shakuntala's mind turned completely blank.

"I rang up the eldest son yesterday, and he agreed that you can stay here. But do keep two bedrooms locked. You don't need so much space anyway. I will open up this small room for you to use, along with the kitchen, prayer room and living room."

Shakuntala stood dumbstruck.

Aunty continued, "I think it will be good for everyone that you and Bharati shift here."

Shakuntala was confused. How could she stay by herself in such a large house? Would she have to cook separately for herself? How would she manage it? How would she feed her daughter?

Aunty asked, "Why are you looking so sad? Do you think I am driving you out of my house? You are stupid. Get rid of those thoughts. You will only sleep and spend your spare time here. You will work in my house throughout the day and eat there too. You may find it difficult to adjust for the first few days, but later you will settle down."

Shakuntala felt reassured.

"The two houses are next to each other. Both of you can stay here happily. If necessary, you can stand in the courtyard and call out to us. When there were people living in this house, we often conversed like this."

After pausing for a while, Aunty said, "The house was crowded when my brother-in-law's family lived here. We celebrated all festivals together. The children got on very well too. They ate and studied together. There was much love and affection among them. It was fun all the time.

"A few years later, my brother-in-law and sister-in-law died in quick succession. By then, the sons were already working in a different city and lived there with their families.

"They sold their land, fields, groves, etc., over the years, leaving only this house untouched. They may sell it too someday."

Aunty gave her the key. "Keep this with you. Clean this place up when you have the time. After that, you can shift with Bharati."

Shakuntala remained glued to the ground.

"What are you thinking? There is nothing to worry about. The house will be neat and clean and maintained when you are here. Besides, you would not need to keep an eye on Liku. He is getting naughtier every day. It is difficult to control him at times. Where did he learn to hit people like that? He often does so with whatever is handy. You saw how he hit Bharati on her head the other day. No one knows what he might do; he is unpredictable. It is impossible to watch the two children all the time.

"That is why I want you to live separately here. Come to our place only for work. The two children will be apart, and Bharati will have enough space to play. She need not be scared of Liku hitting her again."

Shakuntala continued to stand quietly.

"Many other houses in the village are locked up like this one. Sons go away to work and settle down with their families there. Some of their children go abroad to study, and if they do return, they do not come to the village. Therefore, the houses remain locked up. Now bolt the door and come with me. Uncle must have got up by now. He will need his tea. Have faith in God and everything will turn out right."

"Aunty, I have been thinking of telling you something these past few days," interjected Shakuntala.

"Tell me."

"I was alone earlier. Now there are the two of us. Bharati needs so many things. We stayed at the hospital for several days. You must have spent a lot of money. And the child is growing up. Expenses are likely to increase. I was wondering if I could work somewhere else also and earn some money."

"What would you do?"

"I cannot think of anything. I am not very intelligent. But I think the child's expenses could be taken care of if I do domestic chores in a few houses."

"How much do you think you can earn? Will it be enough to take care of both of you?"

"No. I am not saying that. You are paying for everything for us now. I could be of some help."

Aunty did not say anything.

Shakuntala persisted, "It would help if you could find me a job somewhere. You know so many people."

"What do you have in mind?"

"Some shop or office or company. I am prepared to do any work. I have not studied much, but I can work as a peon. I will continue to stay here and do the housework. I will never be able to repay your debt. You have done so much for me."

"That is all right. I too have been thinking about it. I want to find you a job somewhere. We are old and dependent on our children. We cannot do much for you. You had told us when you first came that you didn't need any salary. You only wanted to be fed and clothed, which was not much of a problem. However, that will not do now. The child's expenses will increase gradually, and you surely need some money. Bharati is a girl; you have to think about her future too."

Aunty was lost in thought. Shakuntala too seemed to be in the same state.

"I remember something," said Aunty. "Kuni's cousin set up a college in the marketplace several years ago and is doing well financially. He came to our house the other day and told me that he had recently opened an English-medium school near the college. It is doing well, if he is to be believed. And why shouldn't it do well? No one wants to send their children to Odia-medium schools anymore. There are very few children these days in the village school. I'll tell Kuni to recommend you to her cousin. He might ask you to sweep or watch over the children."

"Yes, Aunty. Please talk to her today. I will do anything I am told." Shakuntala brightened visibly.

"Let him come. Finish the pending work and make some tea for us."

# Chapter 7

It was evening and Shakuntala was in her new house.

She pulled the edge of her sari over her head and lit a few wicks soaked in ghee below the *chaura*, a stone structure with a basil plant where Odia women pray in the evenings.

Bharati was crawling around in the courtyard.

Shakuntala meditated for some time in the prayer room and then stood in the courtyard watching her daughter.

She had cleaned the large enclosed space and Bharati was happily crawling all over it. At times, she tried to walk, though unsteadily. Sometimes, she would just sit down.

Shakuntala sat on the steps and kept looking.

It was quite a big building. There were five large rooms. The courtyard was in the middle. There was a tap in one corner with a cemented platform under it, where one could bathe or wash clothes and utensils. A small drain carried away the overflow. The chaura was in another corner.

Aunty had given her the large room in front of the prayer room. There was a big old-fashioned bed, a sizeable wooden cupboard and a clothes horse. Shakuntala kept her clothes on it and Bharati's in the cupboard. There was a cement slab above it, with two locked trunks. Shakuntala climbed a ladder to dust them. The kitchen was next to the prayer room. It was not very large but spacious enough. There was a hearth in one corner and shelves along a wall on which there were a few containers and bottles. Shakuntala cleaned everything and rearranged them.

The house had almost turned into a jungle. It took her nearly a week to bring everything in order. The prayer room had pictures of gods and goddesses, and she dusted and cleaned them too. When the cleaning was done, she moved in with Bharati with no idea of what the future held for her. She had left everything to the Divine.

Shakuntala stared at the sky. She caressed Bharati and said, "Look, it's Maamaa! Uncle Moon is looking at you and smiling."

Bharati looked up. She cackled and clapped. Wriggling out of Shakuntala's grip, she moved around aimlessly. At times, she just stood and stared upwards, her face wreathed in smiles. Shakuntala felt that Bharati was very happy for the first time.

The moon was full, and its light flooded the courtyard.

Thinking about her past, the young woman found herself wishing to ask the moon several questions.

Suddenly, she heard Aunty calling for her.

Shakuntala picked up her daughter, closed the door and came out.

"Did you call me, Aunty?"

"Yes. This gentleman has come. Talk to him about your job."

Shakuntala stopped in her tracks.

"Why are you standing there? You told me that you wanted to take up a job. I hadn't forgotten and had told Kuni about it. She rang up her brother and spoke to him. He has come and wants to meet you. There is nothing to fear. You cannot live in this world if you are scared of everyone. I had told you about him the other day. Kuni has told him everything about you. You will only discuss the terms of employment."

"Sir, namaste," Shakuntala said with folded hands. She stood with her eyes lowered. Kuni introduced her, "Bhai, this is Shakuntala, about whom I had told you."

"What kind of work can you do?" Satyabrata Babu asked gravely.

"Sir, I will do anything you tell me," said Shakuntala softly, her eyes still lowered.

"Will you sweep and swab the floors at the school?"

"Yes, sir!" said Shakuntala eagerly.

Aunty added, "Take a look at our house. It is she who keeps it sparkling. She can do all odd jobs. You will not have any reason to complain."

"You can start working from tomorrow."

Aunty remarked, "She will do anything you tell her to do."

"There is something else. You have to clean the toilets for the present. The person who was doing it has left. There is another woman there who does it, but it's a bit tough for her to do everything alone. The two of you can work together. Every morning, you have to finish cleaning it before the school opens at eight. During school hours, you will work as a peon. It's a new school, and the employees are few. Therefore, everyone has to perform different tasks."

"Sir, I have a small request," said Shakuntala.

"Tell me."

Aunty said, "Get all your doubts cleared now itself. Ask whatever you want."

"No, sir. I have nothing to ask about the work. I will do all that is given. I accept your terms. I have only one request."

"Tell me. What is it?"

"I would like to bring my daughter to the school every day. I assure you, sir, I will not neglect my duties because of her. You will see for yourself that I will discharge all my responsibilities diligently. Work will not suffer on account of her."

"That's all right as far as I am personally concerned. But ours is a school with many children. I don't know how this is going to work out."

"Don't say no to her, Bhai. She will not neglect her work. Please permit her," said Kuni.

Satyabrata Babu was quiet. He was thinking something.

Kuni continued, "Don't think so much about it, Bhai. How does such a small thing matter? You are the owner. What you say goes. You must employ this poor girl. It would be convenient for both her and us. She will walk a few kilometres to the square and reach the school within five minutes if she takes a bus from there. She can return before evening. She can live here and perform a few chores for us. She has never allowed me to do any work since the day she set foot here. I have turned into an idler now. I will have to do everything if she goes away. And there is Liku to be attended to. You know how naughty he has become. I cannot take care of everything on my own. I am completely out of touch with household work. It will be the end of me if I have to do everything by myself. She is making a small request. Please grant it."

"You are right in your own way. But I run an organisation and have to abide by its rules even if I am the owner. I made the rules for everyone. How can I ask the others to follow them if I violate them? If I permit one person to bring her child to school, others might want to do the same. That will put me in a real fix."

"Nothing of that sort will happen. You are worrying unnecessarily. If Shakuntala brings her child to the school, does it mean that everyone else will do the same? Why should you permit the others? Forget these minor details. Just tell her when to join."

"She can come from tomorrow," said Satyabrata Babu.

"All right. She will be there. Shakuntala, get something for Bhai to eat."

Shakuntala bowed to him and went to the kitchen.

That evening, after she had finished working, she sat in the prayer room for some time with Bharati at her side.

"What kind of life am I leading, O Lord! How many turns has it taken! A new life will begin for me again tomorrow. O Lord! I accept whatever you have ordained. I surrender to you. Your will be done!"

"Ma...Ma..."

Bharati clasped Shakuntala's cheeks and pulled her towards her.

"O Lord! You have tied this small child's fate to mine. You have to ensure that she turns out fine."

She paid obeisance to the deities with tears streaming down her face.

The next day, she woke up much before daybreak. She cleaned the house and took her bath. She took Bharati to Aunty's house and set to work. She had to make breakfast and tea for everyone when they woke up. Shakuntala moved around the house like a machine. She bathed her daughter and fed her. She finished her own breakfast and then packed lunch for both of them. She dressed her and put a large black mark on her forehead.

She selected a sari and stood before the mirror. She could not recall when she had last considered her reflection this minutely while combing her hair.

*"Why should you look in the mirror? You only have to look at me to see yourself."*

*"How does it help me if I look at you?"*

*"Two things will happen. First, I can look at your beautiful face*

*for a long time. Second, I can be your mirror and ensure there is nothing wrong with your appearance." He burst into a hearty laugh.*

Shakuntala was startled.

She pressed her palms to her ears. Why had she been reminded of this snippet of a conversation that happened so many years ago?

She combed her hair and dusted her face with talcum. She wore the sari that Kuni had given her and looked into the mirror again.

"Shakuntala! Shakuntala! Where are you? What are you doing? Come here. It's getting late," Aunty called and came in.

"I am coming."

Aunty shouted out to Kuni to come quickly.

Shakuntala stared at her in amazement.

"What's the matter?" Kuni asked as she entered.

"Look at Shakuntala!" said Aunty.

"Why, indeed! Shakuntala! You are looking really beautiful. I have never seen you like this. Your chignon is fabulous. I am seeing a bindi on your forehead for the first time. The sari sits well on you. You had hidden yourself all this while," Kuni said with a knowing chuckle.

Shakuntala could only smile.

"I had been telling her all along to comb her hair and dress decently. But she ignored me and always looked unkempt. She wears any sari she can lay her hands on. She is busy all the time. How beautiful she looks today! Be like this always. All right! Come. You are getting late. Uncle has called an autorickshaw for you. He will take you to the school and show you the way. He will also meet Satyabrata. You will be on your own from tomorrow."

"Is Uncle going with me?" Shakuntala asked in amazement.

"How will you find your way otherwise? Have you ever been there earlier? Except to go to the temple, you are scared to set foot outside. The only other place you have seen is the hospital. How will you find your way to the school?"

Uncle called Shakuntala from the other room.

Aunty said, "Uncle is looking for you. He is a stickler for punctuality. Let us go. It's late already. He will get angry."

Shakuntala packed a spare set of clothes for Bharati and a few toys.

The autorickshaw moved towards the school. It crossed the serpentine road of the village and reached the embankment. Shakuntala looked at both its sides. Memories arose in her mind. She had followed Uncle to his house one day along this very embankment. There was darkness all around, yet she did not want to go back to what she had left behind. She had to pierce the darkness that was ahead and forge forward. That was why she had blindly followed Uncle without thinking of anything else. She had tried to find a path for herself amidst that darkness. The presiding deity of her village had helped her. She had walked a few steps along that important path that day and was retracing them today.

She was going to work and earn a lot of money, Shakuntala resolved. She was going to provide a decent education to her daughter and make something out of her. She was happy that she was going to work in a school.

She had been a good student at one point of time. She had wanted to study as much as she could and had aspired to become a good teacher. She wanted to contribute to society.

"Why, friend! Such a variety of jobs is available these days. You are such a good student. Why do you insist that you want to be a teacher? Why don't you want to be a doctor? Why don't you become an engineer like your brother? Why does teaching fascinate you?" her friend had said one day when they were both children.

"You are right to a certain extent, friend. I don't want to become an engineer, but I would surely like to be a doctor if I get the opportunity. You know Father's financial condition. He has spent most of his savings in educating my brother. Who will finance my studies in medicine? Therefore, I have decided to become a teacher and help children grow up into responsible members of society. As a teacher, I can also do some social work. Good teachers are needed, and I am going to become one, come what may."

However, fate had ruled otherwise. Her dream of becoming a teacher had remained just that—a dream. She was now going to work as a peon in a school. She sighed and prayed to the presiding deity of her village. She said to herself, "Your will be done!"

"Hurry...hurry...hurry! Who wants to come onboard the bus? It will leave in a minute." Shakuntala came out of her reverie when the bus horn blared.

She looked around herself. She was at the bus stand. She had come here earlier too. That day, she had been so helpless. Shakuntala looked out of the autorickshaw and saw the square from which four roads went in different directions. She had stood there one day long ago and wondered which road to take. She had found the right one by divine grace. God had indeed been merciful! Uncle had arrived like a messenger from heaven. Thank God, she had not lost her way.

"We are at the school, Shakuntala. Stop here, son," Uncle told the driver.

Shakuntala's bubble of memories burst, bringing her back to reality.

She got down and looked around.

It was a double-storeyed building, in front of which many children were playing. She looked at them.

"Come. Let us go inside. I'll find Satyabrata and go back after leaving you with him. Since you have already talked to him, there won't be any problems."

Uncle opened the gate and walked in, with Shakuntala following him.

# Chapter 8

Before setting out to work, Shakuntala gave a few toys to Bharati and made her comfortable. As the day progressed, Bharati flitted between playing by herself and teetering after her mother. She would take a few shaky steps and fall down before smiling and raising herself back up. Occasionally, she would cry and roll on the floor. Her mother would then pick her up and dust her off.

Shakuntala washed up for lunch after finishing the work. She was afraid that someone might cast an evil eye on Bharati. Throughout the day, she had been taking her to a corner and breastfeeding her until the child was full and content and ready to fall asleep.

Shakuntala now laid Bharati down on a mat and covered her. After resuming work, she would occasionally see if the baby girl was all right. She was afraid but could do nothing. She did not have anyone with whom she could leave Bharati. She was all alone and all by herself!

Warm tears blinded her.

She picked Bharati up again, pressed her to her chest and caressed her forehead.

Kumuda sat beside her. She said, "You are showering so much affection that the child's face has turned crimson. This is perhaps your first day here."

Shakuntala nodded.

"It's good you have come. Sukanti used to sweep and swab the floors here with me. She went away a month ago. I was doing all the work alone. I had given up hope of anyone joining in her place. Thank God you have come. It was tough for me as I am getting older," said Kumuda.

"It's also difficult for me to stay at home as my daughter-in-law is a real shrew. I have a son only. I went through tough times to make something out of him. We lived happily until he picked up this girl and brought her home one day. She could not accept the fact that the mother and the son got along very well and therefore made my life miserable. I requested Sir for a job to be away from home during the day," she relayed the rest in one breath.

Shakuntala lowered her head and listened to Kumuda without interrupting. She reassured her, "Don't worry, Aunty. I will do much of the work and make it easy for you."

"Thank you so much. What is this child's name?"

"Bharati."

"Bharati, come to me," Kumuda said, extending her hands towards her.

Bharati turned her head away.

"I am no stranger. Come, we will play and laugh."

Turning to Bharati, Shakuntala said, "Go to aunty and sit quietly beside her. I will be back." She then returned to her work.

The young woman worked tirelessly. She not only finished her own assignments but also about three-quarters of Kumuda's. In her heart of hearts, she was happy that there was someone to look after Bharati and therefore did not mind taking up Kumuda's share. She had promised Satyabrata Babu not to neglect her work even with her daughter being with her. God had been merciful. She could now concentrate on the work with Kumuda looking after the child.

Everyone was pleased with Shakuntala's dedication.

Upon completing the first month, she went to the school office to collect her salary. She was overjoyed. After returning home, she went straight to Aunty and placed the money in front of her. She could not control her emotions, tears flowing out when she bowed at Aunty's feet.

"Why are you crying? Better days are ahead," Aunty said, placing her hand on her shoulder. "Get up! You are working so hard that you deserve to be rewarded."

Shakuntala wiped away her tears.

"Go and change. The child must be hungry. I wonder if she is fed properly at the school. Feed her first. What are you doing leaving the money here? Put it in your cupboard and lock it."

"Let it be with you, Aunty. It is yours. Would this day have ever come if you had not helped me? This is only because of you." Shakuntala's eyes turned moist again.

"That is over now. You have gone through so much hardship, and God has answered your prayers. Spend the money on your daughter."

"No, Aunty. You keep it," Shakuntala insisted.

"Why should I? Keep it with yourself…Fine! It's all right if you want to pay me back for the child's expenses. But I will keep it only for safekeeping. I will take money from you only when Bharati has been educated and settled. Now go and change."

Shakuntala could not say anything more. She picked up the money and went to her house.

Gradually, she adjusted to her new life. Her limbs moved automatically from four in the morning until midnight. She did not rest for even a minute. She made sure that Aunty and Kuni Bhauja were not inconvenienced because of her job at the school. She tried to finish all the chores at home before leaving. At the school, she not only did her work but most of Kumuda's also. The old lady looked after Bharati while Shakuntala worked.

"Oh my God!" Shakuntala squealed one day in spite of herself. Hot gruel had spilled onto her hand as she was trying to make rice quickly.

Aunty heard her and ran into the kitchen.

"What has happened?"

"The rice pot momentarily slipped from my grip and the hot gruel scalded my hand," Shakuntala said as she poured cold water on the injured skin.

"Quite a lot of the gruel seems to have fallen. Your face gives away your agony."

"No, Aunty, it's nothing serious."

"What do you mean it's not serious? Blisters might develop. And it's your right hand. How will you work at the school?"

Kuni too rushed in, reprimanding, "Why are you working in such a hurry? You can leave some of the work for me."

"Don't worry, Bhauja. I will be all right."

"I have been telling you for quite some time not to cook everything before you go. My husband does not like rice in the morning and eats lunch in the canteen. Why cook in such a rush then?"

"Yes. Kuni is right. Starting tomorrow, just make breakfast. If necessary, she can make lunch."

"Aunty! How can I leave everything to Bhauja and run away to the school? I cannot do it."

"Why not? Earlier, all the cooking had to be finished by nine because Debu ate lunch before going to the office. Nowadays, he does not want to eat rice and dal so early. So why cook so hurriedly in the morning? We eat lunch at two in the afternoon.

Why should you work so hard in the morning? You don't have to do it. Cook only for yourself and Bharati."

Shakuntala's morning workload was reduced. She had more time to pray. But she was not happy that she was cooking only for herself and her daughter.

"Aunty! I think I will cook at my place sometimes. Nothing much, just some rice and dal for the two of us to carry for lunch. I need your permission to do so," Shakuntala haltingly said one day.

Kuni had been cooking lunch nowadays, which Shakuntala and Bharati ate after returning from school. Shakuntala had been feeling bad about the arrangement.

"All right. Cook there at times if you feel like it. But you are always welcome here to eat whatever you want. Ask Kuni for anything you need," Aunty finally said.

# Chapter 9

The school where Shakuntala worked was expanding gradually. The children were increasing in number, and the environment there was changing considerably. Shakuntala's situation also changed along with it.

Several new buildings had been constructed for the growing number of children. Hostel facilities were now available near the campus. Arrangements were made to provide breakfast and lunch to the day scholars. The employees' workload had increased considerably, but Shakuntala was always particular about her responsibilities. She kept an eye on the small children too. Often, she cleaned them up without hesitation when they sullied themselves. She knew their needs and helped them whenever they needed something. Two or three people had been recruited, but she had never seen them working diligently. She did not waste time during working hours. She knew that the owner could not keep a watch on her all the time but believed that someone up in the sky was watching everything. He saw, knew, and heard everything.

She remembered what her father used to tell her. "Always remember one thing. No work is unimportant. Whatever you do in life, do it to the best of your ability. God will then be happy with you. He rules over everyone. The entire world will be happy with you when God is happy with you. A person's path is laden with flowers when everyone is happy with them. They can overcome all the hurdles in their way to reach the destination. Of course, this is easier said than done. But we have to work diligently. Nothing should deter us from it," he would say.

The children were the most important in the school. Everything was meant for them, and Shakuntala tended to them with care. They loved her and ran after her, shouting, "Shakuntala Didi! Shakuntala Didi!"

Bharati too had grown up. Her height and weight were increasing. She was now too heavy for Shakuntala to carry to the school. The little girl wouldn't walk such a long distance every day either. These days, Shakuntala did not want to bring her to the school as she would not sit still. She ran after the children and would not let her mother do any work if she were restrained.

Shakuntala had a new problem now and did not know how to solve it. Where could she leave her daughter?

One day, as Shakuntala sat next to Aunty after returning from school, the old lady asked, "Have you eaten after coming back?"

"No, Aunty, I haven't. I fed Bharati and thought I would talk to you for a while."

"What's the matter? Any problem?"

"No. No problem as such but..."

"Come on. Tell me."

"Bharati is growing up. I cannot carry her for such a long distance, and neither can she walk so far. I was wondering whether I could leave her with you when I went to work."

"It's all right. Why do you have to be so apologetic about it? Bharati is no longer a little girl. Finish her daily chores before you go. As she can eat by herself now, she will not be a bother. When you return, she will be playing here."

Shakuntala was reassured.

Aunty said, "Today, I was also waiting for you to return so that we could talk."

"Why? What's wrong?"

"Liku is almost five years old. He hasn't been admitted to any school. Earlier, his parents were thinking of shifting to Cuttack and enrolling him in a school there while staying in a rented house. They have now given up on the idea. I was told that Liku would study here. Satyabrata, who was here some days ago, told them to send Liku to his school. He will be going there from tomorrow onwards. He might feel like a fish out of water in the beginning and might not eat properly. Since you are there, just take care of him."

"Yes, Aunty! This is not a problem. I will take care of him. Don't worry."

"Don't I know that? I have already told Kuni about it. Liku is so naughty that she is worried about him. No one knows what he will do at school. He might get into a scuffle. He doesn't even know how to eat, and neither can he go to the toilet by himself."

"Don't worry, Aunty. I will be there, won't I? Why are you worrying? I will take complete care of him."

"One good thing is that while Liku is at school, Bharati will be here. Liku will be so tired when he returns that he will go to sleep after bathing and eating lunch. He will sleep for a few hours and go out to play when he gets up. You will reach here roughly around the same time. Thus, Liku and Bharati are not likely to fight. Besides, the little girl does not trouble anyone. There is no reason why you should drag her to school with you."

Shakuntala felt restless for the first few days when she left Bharati at home and went to school. Her daughter had always been with her even when she worked. Now she had to leave her behind for such a long time and found herself slightly worried. On top of everything, people at the school asked Shakuntala why Bharati had not come. That worried her even more.

However, she reasoned with herself. There was no other way. She had to work. Who would feed them if she spent all the time with her daughter? She was fortunate that Satyabrata Babu had allowed her to bring Bharati to school in the initial days. This was because he was known to Aunty and Kuni. She prayed for his welfare. She also prayed for the welfare of Aunty and her family. Satyabrata Babu had agreed only because of Kuni's persistence. Of course, Shakuntala completed all her work to everyone's satisfaction. Often, she did more than what was expected of her. She had also been compensated well for her hard work. Satyabrata Babu was happy with her and had made her a permanent employee. Her salary was raised. The teachers, children and other employees liked her. What more did Shakuntala need?

She recalled her mother saying, "Never blame God for anything, my dear. On the contrary, thank Him for everything. They say whatever God does is for the good of human beings. However, we often criticise him because we don't like his handiwork at times. We must realise that all of us are here to serve God. He does his work in his own mysterious ways. We should be patient with a positive frame of mind. Only then can we realise that whatever God does is for our benefit. We should try to adjust to our circumstances and thank God for everything he has given us. Repeat after me: Oh Lord! You have showered so many blessings on me. Never desert me!"

Shakuntala decided to work even harder. She wanted Satyabrata Babu's business to flourish.

# Chapter 10

At night, Shakuntala would often narrate stories to Bharati to make her sleep. She related incidents from her own childhood, tears streaming from her eyes as she took a trip down memory lane. No one knew if Bharati understood what Shakuntala told her, but the child knew that her mother told her new stories every day. It had become a ritual before going to sleep.

Earlier, Shakuntala could talk much nonsense and get away with it because her daughter could not comprehend her words. However, it was increasingly becoming different now; Bharati was growing older and was able to understand what was being said.

The sweet girl had a voracious appetite for new stories every day. Shakuntala had already told her all the ones she knew. How many stories could she weave together after all? Her childhood had been spent in extreme poverty. No one had ever told her stories in her early years. She was not well educated either. Having studied at school only for a few years, she had not heard too many stories from her teachers. To entertain herself as a child, Shakuntala had borrowed some storybooks and read them. But she had to give up her studies after Class VII and had no further relationship with books, given that she was always working. Later on, she never had the chance to read storybooks.

Shakuntala reminisced about her past as she stroked her daughter's hair. She had wanted to study, but her father could not afford it. He ran a small grocery store in the village. There were four children in the house. Their old grandmother, who lived with them, suffered from asthma. Their rheumatoid mother was in bed most of the time. The seven-member family somehow survived on the father's small income.

Shakuntala had never seen her mother in good health. Her limbs were bent. She could not even do her personal chores and often complained about severe pain in her arms and legs. The villagers advised her father to get her treated in the city, but he never had enough money for it.

Father would instead get homoeopathic medicines that were cheap. He also got her a medicinal oil to massage the limbs. Mother somehow made do with them.

Grandmother cooked their meagre food, while Father did the other household work. The family got by somehow. However, Grandmother too began ailing gradually. She was susceptible to colds, coughs, and fever. Her chest filled with phlegm, and she was asthmatic too.

Most of the responsibility of running the household fell on Shakuntala's elder sister, Savitri Dei. She worked without pause from morning to night.

Tonight, Shakuntala was revisiting the past once more for Bharati.

While Dei was the eldest of her siblings, Shakuntala was the youngest. Between them were two brothers. Dei remained so busy with the household work that she never studied. She was enrolled at the village school but never went there. She did not want to go even when there was a temporary respite from the housework. She would hide in someone's house if Father insisted on her going to school. In time, he stopped telling her to study. Their financial condition was not too good either.

The eldest brother, Kanhaiya, was good at studies and went to school religiously whether he got lunch or not. He bought a few books and notebooks with the money that Father gave him and borrowed the others he needed from his friends or seniors who had moved up to the next class.

He was quiet and grave by nature and did not let trivialities bother him. He concentrated on his studies alone. Father was impressed with his diligence, confiding in Mother, "Fortunately, our elder son is really good at studies even though he was born in a poor family like ours. He is serious about them. I am not able to provide him with good facilities, yet he always comes first in class. He will become an important officer one day and help me take care of his siblings. I will see him through school and college, come what may, and ensure that he becomes a reputed officer."

Mother listened attentively, making silent obeisance to the deities.

# Chapter 11

Kanhaiya topped the school in the matriculation examination. Everyone in the village was happy and, persuaded by them, Father got him admitted to a good college in the city.

The younger brother, Ashirvad, however, was not keen on studying. After failing several times in each class, he managed to complete Class VII. He was not willing to study further. Father chastised him, reasoned with him—all to no avail. The son spent most of his time with the unruly boys of the village, smoking bidis and chewing paan. Soon, he took to intoxicants. Everyone in the village was disgusted and often complained to his parents.

Finally, Father stopped talking to Ashirvad. He told Mother that he would not have anything to do with him. Mother too was tired of scolding him. The wayward boy ignored them both.

One day, the police arrested him and some others in a burglary case. Witnesses said he was involved. The police suspected him as he had not returned home that night. They beat him to secure a confession. But it was later proved that he had been drunk that night and had slept on a cemented platform in the village. He was then released.

The family was devastated. Mother cried continuously even after he returned from the police station.

She exclaimed, "My son! We didn't say anything when you stopped studying. You loafed around with ruffians and picked up bad habits. You indulged in nefarious activities. You think of home only when you are hungry. You arrive in time to eat four times a day and disappear after each meal. We put up with even that. But what is this? How have you become a thief? We are poor and going through a hard time. Yet the villagers respect your father because of his good nature. They seek his advice on village and community affairs. But what have you done? Won't you let us live in peace?"

"Didn't you see how they released me when the real culprits were caught? I just talk and play cards with them. That's it! Keeping their company does not mean that I too steal. How can you accuse me like this even after the truth has come to light?"

"Weren't you beaten by the police? This was because you are friendly with criminals. It does not matter whether you are involved in the crime or not. You were considered a thief because you have thieves for friends. Your elder brother studied here and stood first in school. Now, he is doing well in college too. You too are born from the same womb. How could you turn into such a wicked person? I already suffer from several diseases, and you are adding to my misery. You should have thought about me and our poor financial condition. We hardly make ends meet. Your father is the only earning member. How much do you expect him to work? Think about him for a moment. We have to arrange the marriages of your sisters. Do we have the resources? Who will marry them without dowries? But we have to do something. We cannot keep them at home indefinitely just because we don't have money. What will people say?

"Go and assist your father in the shop at least. He will be able to take on some additional work if you do so. You didn't study, so at least manage the shop now. The experience will help you later. You are my darling son! Listen to me. You have already wasted enough time. Think about your future. You might never be able to make amends if it is too late. I have explained everything to you; now, it's up to you. You are no longer a child that I can beat you to make you understand." Mother wiped away her tears. There was so much misery on her face.

Grandmother also spoke to Ashirvad with affection. "Listen to your mother, son. Go and sit in the shop from tomorrow. Don't be unruly anymore. Your father is not able to look after whatever little land we have because he's at the shop all the time. When can he work in our fields? The people who have taken them on lease are dishonest. They give us some paddy or black gram when they feel like it. No one knows how much is harvested and how much is our share. When I was younger, I used to check everything and be present at the harvest. I brought our rightful share home. But that is no longer possible. Those people do as they please."

He listened to them and began helping Father. Though Father would not admit it, he was pleased. Now, the old man could devote some time to the crops.

Father expanded his business now that the younger son was managing the shop well. He set up another shop adjacent to the grocery store and sold potatoes and onions. The villagers persuaded him to sell tea and snacks. They often played cards near the temple, and there was no place nearby where they could get tea. Father agreed as he was confident that his son was there to help him. Moreover, the boy had a head for business.

The situation at home slowly improved.

Father was earning more money than earlier and went to Cuttack and brought effective medicines for Mother and Grandmother.

Everyone at home was happy. Shakuntala was the happiest. She believed that as her father's earnings had increased, he would now let her study further. Like her elder brother, she too would get to go to college. The other two siblings did not study well, but she was as diligent as her brother Kanhaiya.

She dreamt a lot about her future. She would study at the nearest high school after passing Class VII from the village school. She would ride Kanhaiya's bicycle to high school and later join a college at Cuttack. She would study hard and become a good teacher.

She helped her elder sister with the housework but concentrated more on her studies.

Father would go to Cuttack at regular intervals to meet Kanhaiya. Once, she insisted on tagging along. Her brother took her around the college and showed her the hostels, his and the girls'. She was overjoyed and bombarded him with a million queries about college and hostel life.

"Don't ask so many questions," he said, irritated. "Study properly from now on so that you may be admitted here after a few years. You will find the answers to all your questions then. No need to waste your time chatting. Concentrate on your studies."

The advice endured with her all the way back.

Upon reaching home, she happily said, "Father! I hope you will send me to college like my elder brother."

Her father did not answer.

"Tell me, Father! You will send me to college, won't you? I will work hard. I promise you I will secure more marks than he did. You cannot refuse me then."

"I don't have enough money to see one son through college. How can I pay for you too? Besides, he is a boy. He can look after himself anywhere. Can you do so?"

"Why not, Father? Brother stays in the boys' hostel; I can stay in the girls' hostel. I can do everything."

"Maybe you can. But I should be able to afford it. It is easier said than done."

She lapsed into a silence of resignation. Tears welled up in her eyes and her face looked crestfallen.

Savitri, her elder sister, yelled from inside the kitchen, "Father! Why are you breaking her heart now itself? She is a good student. Let her complete matriculation first. Who knows what the future holds for us and her? Our situation is not going to be like this forever!"

"All right! You pass matriculation first. Why discuss all that now? Let the time come. We will see."

# Chapter 12

Elder brother Kanhaiya passed ISC and enrolled himself in Burla Engineering College.

What about Shakuntala's studies? One particular incident could sum up the matter.

The headmaster at her school was an ill-tempered person. He taught mathematics to Class VII. One day, there was so much work to do in the house that Shakuntala could not do her mathematics homework. When she told him so, he hit her on the back, the pain of which would linger in her heart for years!

Later, he called her and said, "A good student like you should not slack off like this. You will do very well if you concentrate on your studies. All our hopes are pinned on you, and I am confident you will make your school proud. Work hard and you will get a scholarship to study further."

That came true. Shakuntala stood first in their area in the Class VII results. Overjoyed, the teachers congratulated her. She was the only one to be able to sit for the merit scholarship examination. The headmaster visited their house the day the results of the scholarship examination were announced.

He turned to her father, saying, "I know that your financial condition prevents you from allowing Shakuntala to study further. I request you to let her study for a few more years.

I have taught Kanhaiya, who was a very good student, but Shakuntala is better than him. She will excel more than her brother if she is given half a chance."

Father agreed with him.

After he left, Shakuntala asked, "Father! When will you enrol me in Class VIII?"

Father kept quiet.

A few days passed. Father never raised the subject. She could not summon up enough courage to remind him but was growing anxious with each passing day.

One day, as she gave him a cup of tea, Shakuntala said, "Father! When will you send me to high school? My friend Tuni told me that the deadline to submit the application is the day after tomorrow. There is only one high school in this area, and there is a heavy rush this year. Tuni said the headmaster was not admitting more students, but he has promised to keep a spot open for me."

Father sipped his tea while she stared at him silently.

"You have had enough of studying. There is no need for more," he said with finality.

Shakuntala was deeply disappointed. Her heart missed a few beats. Hesitatingly, she asked, "Why, Father? Several girls from the village have joined high school. I am not the only one."

"What have you got to do with the others? You should realise our situation is different. Kanhaiya is studying engineering. Do you know how much it costs? Where can I get so much money? The shop is the only income. Fortunately, Ashirvad is assisting me. How do you expect me to pay for your high school and finance Kanhaiya's engineering? I just can't do it because I cannot afford it."

"My schooling will not cost much, Father. I am eligible for a scholarship. It might not be very high but will be a helping hand. Besides, I will borrow the books I need from my friends and will never ask you to buy them for me," she said, sobbing through the words.

"How much money will your scholarship be? It is also not certain when it will be given. It is not easy to get money from the government. And do you think you can manage for several years by borrowing books? You are only a child. You do not understand these things. There is nothing more to discuss. Leave me be in peace.

"Kanhaiya will find a job after he completes engineering. He will contribute towards our expenses. He will repay our loans. You are not likely to get a job even if you study further. Moreover, a highly educated groom will have to be found for you. Where can I find such a person? Even if I succeed, I will have to spend a hefty sum on the wedding. People ask for a large dowry these days."

Tears streamed down Shakuntala's cheeks. She wanted to answer but was not able to bring herself to do so. She seemed to have lost her ability to speak.

Savitri came out of the kitchen and pleaded, "Father! Shakuntala is so keen to study. Why are you disappointing her? I was never good at it, but she has done fairly well. Allow her to study further."

Father only stared at Savitri.

She continued, "How much money will her education cost you? Don't refuse her. Let her continue studying. I will try to economise and save some money from the household expenses."

"Let me think about it for a few days. Go and do your work, and let us not argue anymore."

"What do you mean by wanting to think about it? She says that she has to get enrolled within the next two days," her sister persisted.

"All right then. Let her stay at home for a year. We will send her to high school next year." Father walked away.

Frustration and anger flooded Shakuntala. Her eyes were swollen from crying incessantly. She did not eat or sleep properly for days. She had lapsed into complete silence and talked only to Savitri.

Her sister tried to reassure her. "Why are you working yourself up? Father has only said to wait for a year. You are still young and there is enough time for you to study."

"Dei, do you think I can go back to school after sitting idle for a whole year? Father is concerned only about his son's education, as if I am not his daughter. Perhaps, he found me in a dustbin."

"Forget it. Study at home for a year. You will go back to school then."

Shakuntala stopped arguing; she was exasperated.

She helped Savitri Dei in the household.

Hope still dwelt in her. Father might reconsider after a year and send her to high school after all.

Alas, that did not happen. Father stood firm, and she never set foot in high school. Her studies had ended for good.

Riding the bicycle to school, going to college, and becoming a schoolteacher remained unfulfilled dreams.

Years later, Shakuntala would not have lost face before Bharati had she been allowed to study further as a child.

As a mother now, she struggled to tell her daughter anything new, and the child often got irritated as a result. She noticed that Bharati always wanted to hear fresh stories and new songs. She was curious to know what was happening around the world—a curiosity that Shakuntala could not satisfy. With her limited knowledge, how could she answer all of her daughter's questions? Of course, she had been able to learn a little in the two or three years she had spent working at the large school. She had listened attentively to the teachers' discourse, picking up a few interesting things. Though she had not been able to pay attention to anything except her work on those occasions when Bharati had tagged along! Nowadays, she stood and listened to the speakers at meetings and later repeated what they had said to Bharati. The child was not content with that. She'd insist on knowing more and more.

"Bou, why have you stopped telling me intriguing stories? I don't want to hear those silly tales about princesses, the old demoness, and the ghost on the tamarind tree!"

"What stories do you want to hear?" asked Shakuntala, stroking Bharati's forehead.

"Tell me something new and good. There are so many new things on television. You never tell me anything. You keep repeating the same things all the time."

Shakuntala wondered how such a little girl could think so big. How had she learnt to appreciate the value of knowledge? Of course the children of her generation picked up facts fast. Bharati was making new friends in the neighbourhood and watched television every day in Aunty's house. There was no difference between villages and cities anymore. It was good in a way that she was learning so many new things. This was the age for her to learn about them. Let her make new friends and learn from them, thought Shakuntala. Who else was there at home to teach her anyway?

"Why are you quiet all the time? All my friends have started going to school. When will you send me there?" The young girl's query broke her mother's musings.

Shakuntala was startled. She had always wanted to give Bharati a good education but hadn't found the time to plan well. The girl might not be going to school yet, but Shakuntala should at least have bought some books and a slate for her. How had she neglected that? She was only telling her silly stories every night to entertain and instruct her.

"Why don't you say something, Bou?" Bharati shook her by the waist.

"Oh yes! Why shouldn't you study? You will also go to school."

"Then why don't you get me admitted?"

"You are not old enough yet."

"Dipu, Liku, Pappu, and Sheila are already going. They are studying where you are working. Don't you know it?"

Shakuntala did not know how to reply. She knew that these children had been enrolled in the English-medium school. But could she afford the expense?

Her daughter repeated several times that she wanted to go to school. She did not want to sit at home any longer. She wanted to study.

"Why don't you answer, Bou?"

Shakuntala pulled Bharati towards her. She caressed her, saying, "My darling daughter will not only study but also become a school mistress after completing her education." She pressed her to her bosom and showered love and affection on her.

"I will tell Liku that I will also go to school with them from tomorrow onwards," exclaimed Bharati, sitting up happily.

"No! Don't tell Liku anything for now."

"Why not? Liku always teases me and says I am a stupid girl who doesn't go to school and makes me angry. I will tell him first thing tomorrow that I will also be going to school."

"Let me arrange it first. Don't say anything to anyone at present."

"And what about Liku continuously teasing me?"

"Why are you getting upset? You are not a stupid girl. I will bring books, notebooks, and pens for you tomorrow. A slate and some chalks too. We will first start your studies at home and then you will go to school. It's getting late. Let us sleep now. An important meeting is to be held at our school tomorrow, and I have to go early. You too have to get up with me. Go to sleep. We will talk again in the morning."

Shakuntala closed her eyes and feigned sleep. She ardently wished for her daughter to study a lot and move up in the world. How would she achieve her objective? She had been able to save only a little from her salary so far. Would it be enough? She may not have to spend a lot initially, but it would certainly be needed later. She had to think of everything starting now itself. Who would help her later on?

She ran her fingers over Bharati's head. The child was nearly asleep.

She got up to catch some air out in the open courtyard. Hearing the faint sounds of a band playing at a distance, she recalled that Sanghamitra Aunty's daughter was getting married in the adjoining street. The bridegroom's party was perhaps on its way there. Sanghamitra Aunty had invited her, but Shakuntala had deliberately not gone. She also refused the women of the neighbourhood who had asked her to accompany them. She had finished the work at Aunty's house and returned to her place. What would she have done at the wedding after all? She knew all about marriages and relationships. God had seen to it that she had experienced them.

Shakuntala sat on the steps, travelling back to the past through her mind's eye...

# Chapter 13

"Do you hear, Shakuntala? A very good proposal has come for your Dei," her mother said happily the moment the sisters returned from the riverbank.

"Oh really? From where?" she asked eagerly.

"From a neighbouring village. Dukhi had come in your absence. She left just a moment ago. She has given a good proposal for your sister. The boy is an only son. His father is no more, and his only sister is already married. Only mother and son stay at home. The boy runs a grocery like your father, but it is in the house itself. It's a pucca building. They have landed property and are fairly well-off."

While her mother was going on, Shakuntala stared at Savitri, who had just walked into the kitchen, glancing at the two of them.

"I think we should go ahead. Savitri will live nearby and visit us frequently. You may also visit her when you feel like it." Mother's happiness was effusive.

"All that will come later. Tell Father to find out details about the boy first. You should decide only after securing the necessary information," suggested Shakuntala.

"Your father said that he knew the boy's father. Of course, we do not know much about the boy, but we think he must be all right. Since he belongs to the neighbouring village, anyone can tell us things about him. Your father can go to their house. Dukhi gave the impression that the boy is suitable. Your father and I think we should accept the proposal."

"Have they seen Dei?"

"As he lives in the neighbouring village, he might have seen her somewhere or the other. He must have heard about our family even if he has not seen her. Dukhi said that the boy's mother would come with a ring for Savitri if we accept. They want the marriage to be solemnised as soon as possible. As only the mother and the son live there, the chronically ill woman finds it difficult to cook and manage the house. Dukhi gave me the impression they are in a hurry to get the boy married."

"What do you mean that they are in a hurry?"

"It means that they will solemnise it as soon as possible. They are only waiting for our consent. Let her get married somehow. We will leave her to her fate after that. We are fortunate. Where would we have looked for a groom for her? Everyone demands a fat dowry. God has been merciful to us. She will at least get two full meals a day and enough clothes to cover herself. What more is needed?"

Mother was silent for a while before resuming, "My daughter will live happily. Dukhi described Sura as a decent boy. My daughter will reign there. She will be her own boss as the only sister-in-law is already married and the days of her mother-in-law are numbered. Let her be married, and then I will find someone for you too. I can die in peace after that. You know how my health is. I have no desire to live like this."

Father walked in just then, asking, "Have you begun dreaming about Savitri's wedding already?"

Shakuntala went to the kitchen.

When the sisters went to bed that night, Dei asked, "You don't seem to be very happy about my marriage!"

"No, Dei. Why are you thinking like that? It's wonderful that you are getting married. I should be the happiest of all. You are my only sister, and I will get a brother-in-law who will shower love and affection on me and give me gifts. All this makes me happy. However, I am also sad that I will be lonely and will really miss you. When you go away, my desire to study will haunt me incessantly. Mother says that the marriage will be solemnised soon and that we should take advantage of the fact that the discussion has been initiated by the groom's side. We are not rich enough to wait for better proposals."

"But, you know, I don't want to marry so soon," confessed Savitri.

"Well, girls from poor families like ours do not have choices. We always have to compromise."

"You are right. I have not even studied. Besides, our poverty will discourage prospective grooms. Therefore, I cannot tell anyone whether I like something or not. Father and Mother are happy because I have been accepted for marriage despite my appearance and illiteracy. You are fair and beautiful like Mother, while I am dark like Father. I live here and work right through the day and will do the same there." Savitri seemed dejected.

"Why do you say that? You could not study because of lack of opportunity. You sacrificed your studies for the sake of our family. I have studied only up to Class VII. I could not ever have studied even that much if you had wanted to study. Besides, you are not inferior in any way just because you did not study. You manage the household work and finances well. Is there any girl in the village who is better than you? I wonder how the household will run after you go away."

"You don't have to flatter me. You are no less yourself. You are only a child, but you will do much better than me later on. You are quite intelligent too."

"How does that help me? Had I completed matriculation, I could have taken up some job. Is it a sin to be born a girl, especially one in poverty?" Shakuntala choked on her words.

Both of them became silent.

Savitri's marriage was simple and without much pomp and ceremony. Very few relations and friends had come. Father said that he would invite everyone for his son's marriage and present them with clothes. This time, he had invited only a few people, including those relatives who could go back at night.

Mother kept saying, "It's the marriage of our first child, but we are not able to do much."

"Oh, come on! Don't you understand anything? We have to get the girl married somehow, and you are worrying about the number of guests and doing it in style!" shouted Father.

Mother wiped away her tears and lapsed into silence.

However, Grandmother was outspoken. "This is the marriage of the eldest child, and therefore all the rituals should be observed. They won't cost much."

She did not restrict herself to only speaking her mind. She personally ensured that all the customs were indeed followed. Savitri's dowry comprised a few clothes, a couple of Mother's ornaments, some bell metal utensils, a suitcase, and a large trunk. The groom's family had not made any demands.

All the villagers came to see off Savitri. She cried a great deal. Mother, Grandmother and the neighbouring women also cried with her.

The villagers were profuse in their praise for Savitri.

"She is a very good girl...The best in the village...Her in-laws are indeed fortunate...We have never heard her speak in a loud tone...She did all the work at home...She took care of the guests...Everyone was pleased with her...She is so well behaved...Her nature is even better...Her mother-in-law hasn't just got a daughter-in-law but a priceless diamond."

Grandmother added, "That's the truth. She was the bright light that constantly shone in our house. She has been running the household for several years. My daughter-in-law is bedridden, and so Savitri took on the responsibility of running the house even as a child. Who will cook now? I don't know what this little girl will do," Grandmother said, turning towards Shakuntala.

The young girl did not bother with what she heard. She put her arms around Dei's waist and cried relentlessly. It was becoming difficult to pull her away. She let go only when Father scolded her.

Kanhaiya had not come for the wedding as he had an examination. Ashirvad was supposed to accompany Savitri to her marital home. Shakuntala insisted on tagging along with Dei. Grandmother scolded her, saying, "You cannot go. It is the brother who accompanies his sister. What will people say if you go too?"

Shakuntala persisted. Finally, Sura, Savitri's new husband, said, "She is only a child. Let her come. No one will say anything. One sister will accompany another. Why should anyone criticise it?"

Upon hearing Sura, Shakuntala stopped crying instantly. She felt sure that Sura was a decent man who would treat Dei well.

Shakuntala got ready in no time. Mother told her repeatedly to return in a day or two. "This house cannot run without you now that your elder sister is married. Your father and grandmother can manage things for a day or two at the most, but they cannot do so for long."

Sura showered love and affection on her and Ashirvad. He took them on his motorcycle to the market near the village and bought clothes and gifts for them. Shakuntala had never received such warmth from her brothers. She concluded that Sura Bhai was much better than them. She thought that Dei should have married much earlier so that Sura Bhai could have joined their family sooner. She prayed to the gods and goddesses for his well-being. She was terribly sad when it was time to leave but was told repeatedly that she and Dei couldn't live in one house anymore.

Savitri visited her paternal home once a week with Sura. It was not that she managed her house alone. Sura too was involved closely with everything. He would often advise Ashirvad about improving and expanding the shop. The young man took his new brother's advice seriously.

Mother was overjoyed to have a son-in-law like Sura. She thanked the deities, saying, "I must have prayed a great deal to them in my earlier life. That is how I have now got a son-in-law like him. You can never get such a person these days. My daughter is a diamond and my son-in-law is no less. I have actually got a son in exchange for my daughter."

Father would consult Sura on almost all matters. In a way, the new son-in-law had turned into a guardian of the family.

However, with Savitri having gone off to her marital home, Shakuntala's daily household duties had increased a great deal. Earlier too, she used to help out, but her older sister assigned her simple tasks only. Now she had to do everything by herself. She also had to pitch in a lot at the shop—grinding black gram and rice and boiling and peeling potatoes. She even helped prepare the several curries that were needed as accompaniments to the snacks. That was not all. She had to wash many utensils too.

She remained so busy that she had no idea when morning turned into evening. Her body and mind had become a machine. All she did was work and only work.

Grandmother's illness was a cause for worry. She had another asthma attack after Savitri's departure. Father had done his best to care for her. In spite of her busy schedule, Shakuntala also devoted some time to her. Mother too dragged herself out of bed and tended to Grandmother.

But Grandmother's suffering increased each day. Finally, Father and Sura took her to the medical college hospital at Cuttack, where she recovered slightly. They brought her back, but she soon became bedridden again, dying a few days later. At the time, Kanhaiya had already completed his engineering course and was working in a reputed company at a good salary.

Shakuntala would always remember the day the postman came with the first money order from Kanhaiya. Father was reading the newspaper after lunch and went outside when the postman called.

"There is good news, sir. I will not leave without a good tip."

"What is the good news? I cannot imagine any good news coming my way."

"How can you know? Only I know about it. All right! Sign here first."

"You want me to sign? Why? This looks like a money order. Who sent it?" Father was amazed, inking his signature with trembling fingers.

"That is why I say there is good news for you. Your son has sent you money. Your bad days will be over soon. You sacrificed so much to see him through engineering college. You are being rewarded now," the postman said while counting out the money.

He continued, "Your son now has a company job and has sent you money. You must share your happiness. I am not going from here without a tip."

"What should I give you? You don't know how much I have spent to see my son through his studies. You have grown old working in the village post office and know everything that goes on here."

"Just give me my tip."

Father gave him ten rupees.

He came in with his face wreathed in smiles. Shakuntala had been looking at him from the inner veranda. His face was glowing, and his eyes were moist. He went straight to Mother with the money in his hand.

"This is a great day. I have been rewarded for the sacrifices I have made over the years. My son has sent me money from his first salary. He will support me. It is said that a father is happy when his son grows up and a mother is happy when her daughter grows up. Your daughters have been running the household, giving you leave to rest in bed. And now my son is earning, so his ageing father won't have to work so hard anymore. You too have suffered as I have. I will take you to a good doctor now and get better medicines." Father was emotional.

"O Lord! Let my son live for a hundred years." Mother folded her hands, with contentment writ large on her face.

Shakuntala looked at them.

Father addressed her now. "You are my daughter. You are much more beautiful than your Dei. You are also more intelligent. Look! What I was telling you some time ago has come true. My elder son is now earning. He will help me run this household. I will find a good husband for you and get you married." Father patted her on the head.

She stood without saying a word. The sorrow in her bones struggled to break free. She sighed heavily.

"Don't be so happy just now, Father! Let us see how much he sends in future. Tell your elder son to take care of the home front and release me from these obligations. Let him come here and take charge of things," Ashirvad said, entering the room.

"Listen to what he says! Why are you so jealous? How can he look after the house when he is working elsewhere?" Father lay down.

Shakuntala left the room.

# Chapter 14

Shakuntala's mother used to say, "When God speaks through someone's voice, it usually comes true." Ashirvad's remarks turned out to be foretelling. Money poured in for just two more months before the stream ran dry. Thereon, Kanhaiya did write the occasional letter, but that was his family's only link with him.

Mother often cried. Father was unhappy. He wrote several times to Kanhaiya, telling him to come home. Whenever Sura went to Cuttack, he would ring him up. Each time, he told Father that Kanhaiya was busy and would visit the family in a few days.

One day, Shakuntala and Savitri were chatting.

"How has Bhai become so busy all of a sudden, Dei? He does not have time to write, let alone send money!"

"I, too, wonder about that. Doesn't he realise that Father borrowed a lot of money over the years to finance his studies? Fortunately, our wayward younger brother, Ashirvad, is looking after Father's shop. We would starve otherwise."

"Why does someone like Bhai behave like this? He was so worried about Mother's health earlier. Has he forgotten her?"

"Sura told me he is no longer his old self; he has changed. He does not say it to Father and Mother, thinking they will be saddened."

"Everything will be fine if he comes home for a few days. Someone seems to have brainwashed him. Though I always thought that Bhai was too smart to be swayed by anyone."

Savitri replied, "I think I will tell Sura to find out what is happening. Why doesn't he come, and why does he not send money? What is he doing with all that he is earning? He loved Mother so much and always said that he would get her treated by the best doctors when he found a job and began earning. How could he forget her like this? We don't know the truth and are only making wild guesses."

"You are right. Send Sura Bhai to him."

However, there was no need for anyone to go. Soon after, Father received a registered letter from Kanhaiya.

Respected Father

Please accept my pranam. I have been so busy the last few days that I have not been able to write. Sura Bhai rang me up, which he must have told you about. I have been wanting to share something with you for a while.

I became friendly with a girl in my class at Burla. We both got jobs in the same company. We are in a relationship. I have been staying in their house almost all the time. Her parents now insist that we marry soon. She is their only daughter. They want the ceremony to be performed here. I don't know if you will accept this, but I had to agree. There was no point in refusing. Our village is far from here, and conducting the marriage there would be fraught with difficulties. There isn't even enough space for guests to stay there. It is best that the marriage is performed here.

They are quite rich and will arrange everything. I don't want you to spend money to come here either. After the wedding, I will come home with your daughter-in-law. Tell Mother not to worry; I have found a good daughter-in-law for her. There is no problem with her caste and *gotra*. I have not been able to write to you for a long time. Sura Bhai said that you were worried, but I was busy settling my affairs. I was unclear about what to do. And yes! I am not able to send you any money for now. My earnings are needed for married life. I have to rent a house and buy things to furnish it. I need quite a lot of money to manage my expenses. We will discuss this when I come to visit. I hope you and Mother are fine.

Yours sincerely

It was quite a long letter.

A few tears rolled down Father's cheeks by the time he reached the end. Mother stared at the deities in the sky above. Tears streamed out of her eyes too. She wiped them off quietly.

Ashirvad said sarcastically, "You didn't like it when I told you about what could happen. You endured all kinds of privation and deprived us too—all to educate your eldest son! The results are now before you. He is really intelligent and not stupid like us. He is no shopkeeper like me! He has studied and found a good job. All he wanted was to be rich, and he will become so by marrying the daughter of an affluent person. He is now the son-in-law of his father-in-law. He lives in a large house in the city. Why should he come to our godforsaken village? One can see the sun and the moon through the gaps in our thatched roof. We enjoy moonlight and rain inside the house. You dreamt he would repay your loans, take care of you, marry off his younger sister, buy landed property, build houses, and make us rich! Those dreams revolved around your elder son only! Keep waiting. Your rich engineer-son will take you to heaven in a chariot. Who is concerned with me? I struggle every day to make ends meet. I cannot go away leaving you behind. I will stay here forever with you and Mother and continue living in abject poverty!"

Ashirvad's words stung Father to the core. Picking up his *gamuchha*, he hung the light towel over his neck and went out. He returned hours later in the evening. Mother lay on a mat in the inner veranda. Savitri and Sura sat beside her. Father plonked himself down in a corner.

Shakuntala brought tea for him. "Drink this quickly before it grows cold. I have already heated it twice."

Father looked at her. She sensed he wanted to say something, but she turned around and returned to the kitchen.

There was no news from Kanhaiya after that. No one discussed him any longer either. Ashirvad did not ease up on his sarcasm and unleashed it whenever he got a chance.

A month later, Kanhaiya turned up with his wife. He brought clothes for everyone in the family. Neighbours dropped in to see the new daughter-in-law. The villagers held intense and critical discussions, though on the sly. Kanhaiya stayed for a week. Shakuntala noticed that he was a completely different person now. Accordingly, she treated him and his wife deferentially, as though they were guests, not family. Ashirvad hardly said anything to his brother.

Mother sobbed, exclaiming, "Why didn't you inform us you were coming? We would have arranged a feast. You got married elsewhere. The villagers will not spare us if we do not arrange a feast."

Ashirvad butted in, saying, "Why should they not demand it? We didn't do anything when Dei was married. You had promised a grand party for when Kanhaiya got married."

The elder brother conceded, "All right! The marriage is done. We are here for a week. Arrange a feast any day."

"Yes, arrange it but don't invite too many people. There will be unnecessary problems. Call a few persons and give them a treat," offered Shakuntala's new bhauja.

Father was silent.

Mother replied, "All right! Kanhaiya, give some money to Ashirvad to buy what is needed. Take Sura along with you and buy new clothes for all the relatives."

"Everyone will eat at the feast. What is the need for new clothes? This is an unnecessary expense. All right! Arrange it tomorrow. We are going to Dei's place today."

"Tomorrow? So soon? Can it be arranged? Go to your Dei's place, and tell Sura to come here."

The newly-wed couple made their visit and returned a day later. However, neither Dei nor Sura accompanied them.

"You have told everyone in the village that you financed my engineering studies by borrowing money. You gave birth to me, so you educated me. What is all this money talk then? Dei and Sura Bhai talked only about money before my wife, a stranger to them, all the time we were there. Don't I have any prestige?"

He continued, "I made a mistake going to Dei's house. It looks as if they are the only ones who are worried about our family. I don't seem to have any stake or importance here."

"When did you think of the family? Would you have acted like you have if you had thought about us? Forget it!" Mother's voice was soft but piercing.

"What I have become, I don't know. You make indiscriminate accusations against me! I should not have come here. No one loves me here anymore. I wonder if I have returned to my own house or to someone else's!" Kanhaiya was enraged.

As she walked out, Bhauja said, "I had told you not to come here. How can I show my face to my parents when we go back? What will I tell them about my experience here? I am ashamed."

Mother sobbed before Kanhaiya, saying, "Now you know everything about our situation. Repay the loans taken for your studies. You have fulfilled your duties as a son in the past. Don't disappoint us now. Did I give birth to a son and educate him for this day? Aren't you that same darling child, Babula? How could you change like this? We don't mean anything to you. Everyone else in this world is your own now!"

He left the room without saying anything further and made ready to depart the next day. Shakuntala served breakfast to her brother and sister-in-law. Bhauja pulled her towards herself and slipped a small ring on to her finger. She also gave her a pair of small earrings.

"Keep these. I have given only earrings to your Dei. Don't give the earrings to anyone. Wear them yourself."

Shakuntala accepted them without any argument.

When he touched Mother's feet, Kanhaiya gave her a packet of currency notes. "The feast was not held. We are leaving as I have much work. We will go to Darjeeling for a few days. We haven't gone anywhere after marriage. I cannot go once my leave is over. Keep this money. Use it in any way you see fit. Don't worry unnecessarily. Everything will be fine. Take care of yourself. Your daughter-in-law will send you money every month for your medicines."

Glancing at Shakuntala, he said, "Tell me when her marriage is finalised. I will send the money."

Father sat quietly inside the house.

Kanhaiya and his wife left.

# Chapter 15

Ashirvad worked hard and expanded the grocery shop, with sales going up simultaneously. He engaged a boy to assist Father and set up a much larger shop at the marketplace. His earnings improved, and he converted their thatched house into a pucca building.

There was running water now. A bathroom and toilet were added. The kitchen was rebuilt. He also got a gas connection and stove for cooking.

Meanwhile, there was no news of Kanhaiya. He did not send money for Mother's medicines. The domestic environment was also changing. A severe backache prevented Father from spending much time at the shop. His stomach, too, ached constantly. While he spent most of his time sleeping, Mother seemed to be caught in a perpetual lookout for someone.

Savitri had children of her own by now, and her visits reduced.

A few days later, some more disconcerting news took the parents by surprise.

One evening, after dinner, Ashirvad turned to Mother and said, "Bou! I am getting married tomorrow at the Shiv temple in the adjacent village."

"What?" the parents responded in unison.

"Yes. The girl hails from a village on the other side of the river. I met her when I went there to attend the wedding of a friend. I liked her. We have been meeting in secret for six months now. I cannot do this any longer, and so I have decided to marry."

"Why didn't you tell us earlier? You are telling us just one day before the wedding. Don't you think we have a right to know about the girl and the family?"

"How would it have helped if you had known earlier? The two of you think only about Kanhaiya and have no time for anyone else. Bou, you come with Father and Shakuntala to the temple tomorrow."

"Have you informed Dei and Sura?"

"I will tell them in the morning."

"Do whatever you want. We have nothing to say."

"Why are you sulking? Kanhaiya did not inform you about his marriage and just landed here with his wife. He stayed for a few days like a guest and went back. I am not behaving like him! What have I done wrong? Should one follow a code of behaviour and decorum all the time just to keep you happy? Besides, why should we incur so much expense by marrying at home? At the temple, everyone will get prasad, and that will be the end! The girl's family will arrange it. Tell Father to bring a few neighbours with him."

While Mother was quiet, Father stated with finality that he would not attend.

Savitri later reasoned with him. "Father! Don't be so obstinate. How can you stay away from such an important function? He is not going away like Kanhaiya. After his marriage, he and his wife will be staying here. You must attend. You know your sons well. His wife will take him away from you if you do not forget and forgive. He may be a young fool, but how can you also act in the same way? Go, Father! Invite a few neighbours and go."

When Shakuntala arrived at the doorstep of her acquaintances, their comments were scathing.

"How shameless! Why do your brothers behave like this? The elder one married an unknown girl and went away with his wife. In addition, you people did not even host a feast for the villagers. What is the second one doing getting married today itself and that too in a temple? This is not done. Your brothers are really arrogant. None of them thought about their poor parents! They did as they pleased!"

Shakuntala took their criticism in her stride. She invited them politely and returned home.

While she went with Father and Sura to the wedding, Savitri stayed back with Mother.

They returned after a few hours along with the new daughter-in-law. Savitri performed the customary welcome.

Father had dreamt big. He had wanted to throw a grand feast for all the villagers on his elder son's wedding day and present his relatives with new clothes. His dream remained a dream.

Shakuntala addressed her second sister-in-law as Lily Bhauja.

Lily began controlling the house from day one. She ran it as she pleased, and everyone had to accept that. Shakuntala, too, now consulted with her sister-in-law before doing anything. Regardless, Lily was a difficult person and quarrelled with everyone at the slightest pretext.

She would say, "Those who succeeded in going away are happy, but we are stuck here. One person earns, and the others depend on him for everything. How much can he earn? We have our own future to think about! We are not able to save anything!"

She was extremely disrespectful just because she was the wife of the bread earner. Shakuntala's parents could do nothing but listen to her harangues. They survived on whatever their daughter-in-law offered them. They knew very well that they could not quarrel with her.

For a time, Savitri visited them quite frequently. The visits gradually reduced as the atmosphere at home deteriorated. Shakuntala was the only one on whom Lily could vent out her anger. She too could not do anything but complete all her chores quietly and stay away from her. She would go to her friend's house sometimes. Her friend's elder brother had married almost at the same time as Ashirvad. They talked about the friend's sister-in-law, Surabhi Bhauja, who was quite well behaved. She had studied a lot, and her knowledge was vast. Shakuntala loved to talk with Surabhi, who told her of many things from all over the world. She had no idea that the relationship between sisters-in-law could be so pleasant. They got along like two old friends. Surabhi often combed and plaited her sister-in-law's hair, who in turn made Surabhi's hair into a chignon.

Surabhi did not allow her sister-in-law to work and helped her focus on her studies. She did not allow her mother-in-law to do any work either. Her husband was a bank officer at Sambalpur and came home on weekends. Surabhi cooked delectable dishes when he was present. All of them sat and ate together. They praised Surabhi Bhauja's cooking. Her parents, brother, and sister would visit at regular intervals. Shakuntala marvelled at the festive atmosphere that prevailed in the house. She could not believe what she witnessed. She thought of a poet who had aptly said, "That house where love and affection abound is more beautiful than heaven."

Lily's harsh behaviour and stinging comments offered a stark contrast. At times, it was intolerable. She was angry with

Shakuntala whenever she chatted with Surabhi and tried to hinder their friendship by loading numerous chores on her. Lily would retort angrily if her sister-in-law protested. Shakuntala's parents cautioned their daughter to just keep quiet.

One day, Savitri came home.

She wanted to return after meeting her parents, but they persuaded her to stay for a few days since she was visiting after a very long time. Savitri saw the situation at home, especially Lily's treatment of Shakuntala. Worried, she said, "Our parents will tolerate anything that their daughter-in-law tells them. But what is your crime, and why should you take so much rubbish from her? You have been working almost round the clock and are treated so shabbily. This house does not seem to have a protector!"

Then she told Father, "I am taking Shakuntala with me for a few days. Diwali is approaching. My sister-in-law is coming with her children. Shakuntala is made to work here continuously. She too is a human being. I am scared to come here because of what is happening. Since you had not visited me for long, I was restless and came.

"This is no longer a house; it is hell. You seem to have resigned yourself to the situation, but why should this poor girl suffer? She had pleaded to study up to Class X. She could have passed IA and BA privately later on and taken up a job by now. But see what has happened. You think only about your sons. This poor girl has suffered, and you have forgotten that she has a future too." Savitri expressed her anger and helplessness for the first time.

"Who is telling your sister to work? You think I cannot manage without her? Take her with yourself and keep her in comfort. Take her away and build her future," Lily said quite caustically.

"Come, Shakuntala. Pack whatever you need."

"Father and Mother are here. How can I leave them? Who will look after Mother? How can you talk like that?"

"Leave them to their son and daughter-in-law. You don't have to stay here and do all the work."

Mother addressed Savitri, "You are right, my dear. Take her. She has already suffered terribly. We will manage somehow. Tell Sura to find a decent boy for her. Father cannot move around, and her brothers neglect her. Only Sura and you can do something. Once she is married, I can die peacefully." Mother nearly broke down.

Father also told Shakuntala to go with Savitri.

Once she arrived there, Shakuntala realised how happy she was to be in Savitri's house. Her children loved her and the two-year-old son ran after her on wobbly feet, shouting, "Aunty, Aunty." Shakuntala became one with them. She listened to songs on the radio. Dei told her to do the cooking, saying, "Sura is tired of eating what I cook. You are a better cook than me. He will like the change. I have to rush through the cooking because I have been doing all the housework alone since my mother-in-law died. I also have to tend to the two cows and chickens. As my son clings to me all the time, Sura often has to do household work, but he is not happy about it."

Shakuntala soon learnt what the people in her Dei's family liked to eat and cooked accordingly.

Sura Bhai loved the food she served. He said, "Shakuntala, my sister Sumi and her children are coming for Kali puja. They will enjoy the food cooked by you. They will not stay here for more than a few days if they eat what your Dei cooks."

The children burst into laughter.

"Dei is not such a bad cook," Shakuntala said in mock anger.

Savitri responded, "Let him say what he will. Who bothers? I will see who will cook for him when you go back."

"Let us eat some decent food for as long as Shakuntala is here. You too enjoy it. You have cooked for a long time; let us now enjoy what she makes. Tell me one thing, Shakuntala, I love your Dei a lot, don't I?"

"Don't I know it?"

Dei said, "Forget it. Let's eat."

Sura Bhai did not let the conversation end. He continued, "Who else loves you more than me?"

Savitri replied, "It is Shakuntala. She loves me the most."

"Does she love you more than me?"

"How can I compare you with her?"

Shakuntala was happy to see Sura's deep adoration for Dei. She thanked God that Savitri was a happily married woman.

# Chapter 16

Kali Puja was celebrated with much fanfare in Sura's village. Mother Kali was not worshipped in any other village in that area. But Sura's community believed that the goddess fulfilled all wishes. A large fair was organised for four to five days. Many itinerant vendors sold sweetmeats, household appliances, cosmetics, and assorted items. Practically, all the villagers had guests who had come for the fair. A festive atmosphere prevailed.

Shakuntala had experienced Kali Puja in Sura Bhai's village once before, but the young woman had spent only a few hours there. This was going to be the first time that she would enjoy the entire Kali Puja proceedings.

There were guests in Sura Bhai's house too.

Dei's sister-in-law, Sumi, and her two daughters and son had arrived, along with Ruli, Sumi's sister-in-law. Shakuntala was in the kitchen from morning until night. She cooked all the meals with enthusiasm. She also made sweetmeats as well as *pithas*, a typical Odia cake prepared using rice and sometimes a mix of different types of dal. The families were all praise for her cooking.

The guests were extremely pleased with her behaviour, expertise, and conduct.

Sumi told Savitri, "Bhauja! Your sister is a wonderful cook. She cooks such a variety of tasty dishes; we really enjoyed them."

"Get ready, Shakuntala. Go to the *jatra*." Savitri wanted her to accompany her guests to the open-air theatre.

"Oh yes. Otherwise, you will complain later that we did not allow you to see it," Sura remarked with a chuckle.

Dei shot back, "Why do you always tease her?" Everyone laughed.

Shakuntala went with Sura, Sumi, and Ruli to the jatra.

The next five days went by amidst fun and frolic. Finally, the guests were ready to go back.

As usual, Shakuntala prepared breakfast for everyone that morning.

"Bhauja! You never told us you had such a wonderful sister. I have come here several times after your marriage but have never seen her. Have you kept this beautiful girl hidden? She is not only beautiful but also very nice. What does she do? Is she studying?" queried Ruli.

"Where does Shakuntala study? How old is she?" asked Sumi.

Sura Bhai explained, "She could not study much because the family is not well off. One brother got married to a colleague and went away, and the other one and his wife stay with Shakuntala's parents. The wife's behaviour is bad and unruly, and therefore we have stopped visiting them that often. Savitri goes once in a while to see her parents; I do not go. She was there a few days ago, and seeing how Shakuntala was being ill-treated by her sister-in-law, she brought her here for a change of scene."

"So she stays at home and does not study?"

"Yes! She does not study any longer. She was the topper in Class VII. She earned a scholarship for further studies, but her father did not send her to school after that. She has been at home since then," Dei said, sadness clearly audible in her voice.

Ruli noted, "If she was a good student and the family finances forced her to give up her studies, how can that be held against her?"

Sumi spoke in the same vein. "How does it matter if she could not study much? She has many other skills and is intelligent too. She works diligently without complaining. The best part is that she is always smiling. She never speaks without a reason. Bhauja! Your sister is a gem of a girl! What more does one need?" She smiled and glanced at Ruli Dei.

Ruli too glanced at Sumi meaningfully.

Shakuntala served tea to everyone.

Sura got up. "It's time to leave. The autorickshaw is waiting."

Bidding farewell with respect, Shakuntala touched the feet of all the adults.

Suddenly, Ruli put a five-hundred-rupee note in her hand. Shakuntala was taken aback. Ruli had already given some money to Savitri's children. Why was she giving her money? She did not understand.

She looked at Dei, who merely said, "What's wrong? Why are you confused? Ruli Dei has given you the money out of love. You are also a child like the others."

Smiling, Sumi asked, "Ruli, tell me why you have given money to Shakuntala?"

Savitri and Shakuntala were stunned on hearing the reason. "My sister-in-law has not given the money for nothing. She has an axe to grind," Sumi said, continuing to smile.

Savitri stared in amazement at the two women.

"Bhauja! My sister-in-law is so pleased with your sister that she has accepted her as her daughter-in-law. She will make a formal proposal if you and Sura Bhai agree. She will confirm it as soon as she reaches home. However, there is no need to wait until then. As far as she is concerned, it is final. Only your approval is required."

"What can we say?" asked Sura.

Lines of worry spread across Sumi's forehead. She said, "Why don't you say something, Bhauja? Is something wrong?"

"No, no! Nothing is wrong. This is indeed good news. Sumi, I do not know how to thank you. My parents wanted Sura to find a suitable boy for her. They have given us that responsibility," Savitri said somewhat nervously.

"Then it is even better, Bhauja. You have found the boy now. Anyone would happily accept your sister as a daughter-in-law. Ruli has done just that. Now it's up to you."

Savitri looked at Sura.

"Why are you looking at me? Are such things decided in haste?" Sura seemed irritated. He continued, "Let Ruli discuss it with her people, and you talk to your parents. We will see after that. Sumi! Get into the autorickshaw. It's getting late, and the driver is grumbling."

"All right! We are going now. One thing is certain, Bhauja. The matter is final as far as Ruli is concerned."

The guests went away. Shakuntala stood holding the five-hundred-rupee note.

# Chapter 17

Savitri and Sura continued discussing the proposal.

"Talk it over with your parents first. Ashirvad is also there. He is now more or less the head of the family," Sura said the moment they went into the house.

Savitri responded, "What will Father and Mother say? You know Mother. She was only physically handicapped earlier, but now her new daughter-in-law has turned her into a mental wreck too. Father's will does not prevail. My brother has reduced him to a non-entity. And the less said about his wife, the better. My parents depend on them to stay alive.

"Mother has got two gems for daughters-in-law. One visited her once and then forgot about her and our family. She has bought the elder son. The other daughter-in-law tortures Shakuntala constantly and makes her work like a servant. My sister is permanently depressed. I cannot see her in this state. The poor girl's serious desire to study was crushed. If she is married, she may find some release from her misery."

"Shakuntala is too young to be married now. Let's wait for a few more years. Other proposals will come. She is beautiful and talented. We will find someone nearby. We have not seen Ruli's house or her son. Neither do we know anything about him," reasoned Sura.

"I don't know what can be done for Shakuntala. I have a feeling that her future is bleak. The day I was bringing her here, Mother requested me earnestly to find a husband for her. My parents suggested that you also look around. Shakuntala is no longer young. She has been managing the household for a long time. She is proficient in all domestic matters. She even looks after our children. Why do you consider her to be too young?" asked Savitri.

"We have to think of everything before finally deciding."

"What do you mean? Ruli is Sumi's sister-in-law. They must be decent people. She stayed in our house for five days, didn't she? We know that her husband works in a company and that they have three sons. The eldest one is married. Shakuntala is being considered for the second one. Sumi told me that he too worked in a company even though he has not studied much. What more do we need? Shakuntala is capable of managing a large household."

"Speak to Father first." Sura seemed annoyed.

"I will certainly talk to him, but we must accept this proposal. Do you think Father, being in his situation, can find a decent bridegroom for Shakuntala? She is lucky that the groom is someone within the family and that the proposal has come from them. We should not miss this opportunity. What happens next is her fate. It is Mother Kali who brought her and Ruli here together for Kali Puja."

Sura stared at Savitri.

A moment later, she said, "Do this. Sumi will reach home tomorrow morning. Go to the market and ring her up to find out if they are serious. Make it clear to her that we cannot afford dowry. Being decent people, I am sure they will agree. It is better that everything is made clear at the beginning itself."

"Go alone and talk to Father while Shakuntala is here. She can go later," offered Sura.

"No. I will take her with me and talk to her on the way. I will stay for a night there. I will take our younger child and leave the older one with you."

Soon, Shakuntala returned home with Savitri.

The elder sister related the proposal to the family. Mother was pleased. She said, "God will bless you both for having done so much for us and standing by our side even though our sons have neglected us."

"Shut up!" Father shouted at her. "You still talk about your sons despite how they have treated us. I should never have spent all my money on educating that scoundrel; rather, I should have educated my daughters."

Ashirvad butted in, "What are you blaming me for? I have not abandoned you. My wife cooks and feeds you. How can you equate me with Kanhaiya? You had expected him to support you; now see how he has ditched you!"

"God knows how you are looking after us," murmured Father.

"What did you say?" retorted Ashirvad.

"Forget it. Concentrate on what we are discussing." Savitri tried to reason with Father and Ashirvad.

Father said, "What can I say, my dear? Sura and you have to take care of everything."

Ashirvad shouted, "Tell Sura Bhai to ask your elder son how much he will contribute for Shakuntala's marriage, Father. If he does not want to, he need not come. He had promised to bear Shakuntala's marriage expenses." Lily nodded in agreement.

Savitri asked, "How much can you contribute?"

"What do I have? I am no engineer earning a fat salary. I don't have an earning wife either, Dei! Why do you always pick on me?"

When they were in bed that night, Savitri nudged Shakuntala. "Why were you so quiet when we were discussing your future?"

"What can I say, Dei? As far as I am concerned, nothing is going to change. I work here and will work in someone else's house. Do I have a choice?"

"What a stupid thing to say! What do you think about the boy?"

"What do I know about him or his family? To be frank, I have never thought about marriage. I cannot even think of it in view of the situation here.

"I have seen several marriages in the village. Brides are taken to the river in a palanquin with music after oil and turmeric paste is applied on them. They go to the temples to conduct puja. They are hosted in various houses. I remember my friend's marriage. She had requested me to stay with her for three days, but could I have gone? I was able to go to her only after finishing my work here.

"I was also smeared with turmeric paste along with my friend. I went with her to the river and the temples and sat near her on the marriage dais. After the ceremony, she went to her marital home and returned eight days later. She talked non-stop about her husband and his parents, brother, and sister. I never dreamt that I could also have that experience."

"Start dreaming from today then, stupid girl!"

Sura came the next day. He said he had spoken to Sumi along with Ruli's husband, who had all agreed with whatever he had told them. "They do not want any dowry but want the marriage to be solemnised soon. As they cannot come such a great distance for the engagement, they wish the engagement and the marriage to be conducted simultaneously. The eighth day of the next month is the last auspicious date of the current marriage season. After that, the auspicious period will resume in six months. Their elder daughter-in-law is expecting, and therefore they are in a hurry."

Savitri was overjoyed. "See! My sister is so lucky. My sixth sense told me that this marriage would go through smoothly. We will not wait for six months."

"All right! Give your sixth sense some rest. We should begin making the arrangements. There are only ten days left. We have to hurry."

Several rounds of discussions revolved around the fact that though no dowry would be offered, there would still be other expenses. Who would finance them? Lily was working herself into a fit.

"Who does anything in this house? Those who chose to live elsewhere are enjoying life. Everyone picks on us when something has to be done. Let the marriage not be held. Father doesn't have anything of his own. How can Shakuntala be married?" Lily's tirade in the kitchen could be heard by all.

Shakuntala continued working silently.

Savitri stood near the kitchen door and spoke in a serious tone to Lily. "Listen to me! You have taken enough liberties with Shakuntala. She has taken all your torture in her stride and never retaliated. From today onwards, you will not say anything to her.

"If you do," she continued, "I will take her to my house and arrange the wedding there. You will have to put up with the comments of the neighbours later. And the same goes for everyone else in this house."

Shakuntala came out of the kitchen. "Come, Dei, and sit with Father. I am bringing tea." She tugged at Savitri and had her seated with their parents and Sura.

Just then, Sura announced he would go to the market and make a phone call to Kanhaiya. He would inform him about the marriage and remind him about the money.

Mother said, somewhat haltingly, "One more thing, Sura. Ask Sumi if they are willing to solemnise the marriage at the Laxmi Narayan temple here. It would be cheaper than doing it at home."

"Oh yes! I forgot to tell you. I have not discussed the matter with Ruli directly but have broached it with Sumi, who gave the impression that they would not be willing to hold the marriage ceremony in a temple. Ruli desires that the marriage should be held in a mandap, as per the Vedic rites. They also want the newly-weds to ride in a palanquin. The groom too will arrive in one."

Worry spread across Father's visage. He said, "They will certainly arrive here a day or two before the marriage. We will have to find a place for them to stay and provide hospitality to the guests."

"I had not thought about it," said Savitri as she looked at Sura.

He stated, "There is nothing to think about. Sumi will take care of everything on their side. My responsibility begins when they reach here. I have planned everything. They will stay in our house and conduct all the groom's rites there. They will come in a procession from there to the temple here."

Savitri laughed and said, "What a coincidence! Both of Mother's sons-in-law will come out of the same house! You started your marital journey from there as the bridegroom once upon a time. Will Shakuntala's groom now also make this pivotal beginning from there?"

Ashirvad seemed worried. "Stop laughing! Do you have any idea how the expenses are likely to increase heavily? We have to arrange the procession, band, firecrackers, lights—everything!"

"Why are you so worried? They will stay here. We have to make arrangements, as they hardly know anyone here. What's the problem? Don't you have any responsibility towards your sister? Your business is doing well. You have so much money. Do something for your family."

"Sura Bhai always finds it convenient to criticise me. Who else is doing everything for the family if not I?"

Sura got up to leave. He said, "Yes! You are doing everything. No one denies it. Do some more now. I need to go and speak to Kanhaiya."

Mother told Savitri, "Go back to your house today. But come tomorrow with the children. Nothing will go right if you are not around."

She replied, "Who is going to look after my house? Who will look after my cows? I will take care of everything there and come here when required. Don't worry."

# Chapter 18

Marriage!

The Creator plants dreams in the minds of human beings and marriage is one of them. Had Shakuntala ever dreamt about it? What kind of marriage was she looking forward to? She had seen several marriages in the village but none had left any impression on her. However, she did get married on a dais after observing rituals for two days. Seven married women, including Savitri Dei, smeared turmeric paste on her. She went to the river in a palanquin to bathe. She visited the temple and bowed to the deity. The groom finally arrived in a palanquin, accompanied with a band and firecrackers.

The entire village came out to see her groom. A priest recited mantras; her hand was tied with that of the groom; she wore bangles and had vermillion applied in her hair parting. Though everything was kept low key, all the rituals were observed faithfully.

There was no dowry. Shakuntala's mother gave her a thin gold chain and a pair of earrings. Savitri gave the bridal sari, four bangles and a ring. Lily gave her two bangles thinly coated with gold and a few ordinary saris for home wear. Shakuntala went to her marital home with her belongings in a large trunk, along with a few bell metal utensils.

Savitri and her husband did everything. Sura had informed Kanhaiya about the upcoming nuptials, but the latter had said he could not come because his wife was expecting. However, on Sura's nagging, he later sent some money. With it, Sura bought a gold chain, a ring, some clothes and shoes, and an umbrella for the groom. Though Kanhaiya did not come, his money was of great help.

Savitri held Shakuntala in a tight embrace and cried a great deal when she was leaving. She told her to accept what fate had ordained. "Don't expect too much. We have not been able to give them anything. Take it in your stride if anyone comments about it. Don't be depressed. You are a good girl. Everyone will praise you for your behaviour and hard work in the long run."

She touched the feet of Father, Mother, Sura, Ashirvad, Lily, and the women of the neighbourhood before leaving. Mother dragged herself to the doorstep to catch a last glimpse. She wiped away her tears. The neighbours later said, "Shakuntala is a lucky girl to have got a good husband and good in-laws. She is also the most beautiful girl in the family and almost a replica of her mother. Husband and wife make a handsome couple. He seems to be a fine person. The girl is indeed fortunate. She has suffered a great deal but will now be happy."

Amar was a handsome, quiet, and educated young man. Shakuntala was married to him in the presence of all the deities and the sacred fire. He was her god for the present life and hereafter, tradition said. Her husband! Her life partner! She had heard that marriage was a union of two souls, two lives and two minds. Would it happen for her?

An unknown fear that had gripped her before the wedding now started to fade away. Amar was not lame, blind, or hunchbacked. Though she had not seen him before marriage, everyone had reported that he was handsome.

Amar touched her for the first time when the edges of their clothes were being tied together, as per the custom, during the ceremony. His hand was warm and full of conviction. She wondered if he was holding her more tightly than necessary but accepted it quietly.

Later on, tea spilled on to her hand as she took the cup absentmindedly from Amar. "Ouch!" she exclaimed. She noticed he was genuinely worried. He soaked his handkerchief in water and pressed it on her hand. The experience was enjoyable. On her way to her marital home, her feet got entangled in her sari as she stepped down from the train and walked to the vehicle that had come to pick them up. Her father-in-law and brother-in-law walked ahead. Amar was beside her. Finally, her mother-in-law, Ruli, welcomed them at the door and took them inside.

There wasn't much fanfare at Amar's house. Only a few relations and friends were present. The family, including Sumi and her husband Chitta, were there.

Amar was the second of three brothers. His elder brother was married. His wife, who lived with her mother-in-law, was expected to deliver soon. Therefore, she had not accompanied the baraat. A small feast was arranged the following day. Her sister-in-law gave her a red silk sari to wear. Shakuntala combed her hair and tied it up into a loose chignon. She applied kajal and lipstick and added a spot of vermillion on her forehead.

Shakuntala sat before the mirror and wondered if the image that stared back was really hers. She had never known she was so beautiful, never seen herself looking like this! She knew nothing about lipstick and bindi. Until this day, she had tied her hair in plaits before bathing. At times, she would make it into a chignon. That was all the luxury she had allowed herself in her parents' home. She was amazed at what she saw now and could not believe her eyes.

She had no idea how long she sat before the mirror.

Her sister-in-law hollered, "Are you finished? You only had to put on some vermillion. What is taking you so long? We are getting late."

The young bride hurried out, visibly embarrassed.

# Chapter 19

Very few people had come for the feast; though once they arrived, they surely appreciated Shakuntala's beauty.

Later, her sister-in-law took her to the corner room near the staircase and told her to sit there. "I'll find Amar. He stays on the roof until midnight. Therefore, he likes this room near the staircase. He goes up whenever he feels like it and comes down to sleep late. No one knows when he is on the roof and when he is in his room." She went out, closing the door behind her.

Shakuntala heaved a sigh of relief. She removed the sari's free end covering her head and loosened her hair. She turned up the fan to full speed and sat under it, with her hair flowing all over her face. She went to the window, parted the curtains, and looked out. Moonlight was everywhere. She remembered that she had sat on the steps outside her house in her village and seen the moon several times but never felt the affinity she felt now. She never knew that it had so much magnetism; she wanted to chat with it.

There was a small garden outside the window. It appeared hazy in the streetlight. She thought the scene was beautiful. She turned and looked around the small room. The bed—not very large—was near a window. A new white bedsheet with a floral motif was spread on it. Two bouquets of red roses were on the pillows. A few white flowers mixed with rose petals lay strewn on the bed. The dressing table looked new. She stood before its large mirror and inspected herself minutely again. She loved her image and felt she would never get tired of staring at it.

There was a small study table on the other side of the bed. A few books and a table lamp were on it, along with a bottle of water and a glass of milk. A picture of Lord Jagannath hung on the wall. There was a large cupboard against the wall on one side. She opened it and saw that Amar's clothes were kept neatly, with a few shirts on hangers. Two shelves were empty. She closed the cupboard and returned to the bed.

It was her wedding night!

Had she ever dreamt about it?

No! The answer was a straight 'no'!

Of course, she had heard a great deal about it from her friends Mini and Bina. She recalled all that now. They had talked about their husbands and their families. They had also described how the nuptial bed had been decorated and what their husbands had told them. They narrated everything in the most minute detail.

Shakuntala now immersed herself in those memories...

"Shaku! Hey Shaku! Where are you?" Her closest friend Bina had called out to her one day.

"Coming! Just a moment!" she replied from the kitchen.

Bina came in.

"Why did you come here? Let us go outside. It is hot here," said Shakuntala.

"Come with me. We will go to our place. I have come for only a day. Who knows when we will meet again?" replied Bina.

Shakuntala could not leave then itself because she had not finished cooking.

After waiting for a while, her friend told Lily, "Please cook the rest. I am taking Shaku to my house." Bina dragged her away without waiting for an answer.

Another friend, Mini, was already there.

Bina and Mini had got married on the same day.

Shakuntala now observed them in turns. "Why are you staring like that?" Mini shook her by the shoulder.

"I am looking at both of you. Bina looks beautiful in her Banarasi silk sari, and you are looking lovely in your Sambalpuri silk. I saw you both eight days ago. You look beautiful wearing these saris and ornaments. The vermillion on your forehead and the bangles on your wrists have changed you completely. The sari, bangles, and vermillion really transform a woman entirely. God's creation is wonderful indeed!"

"The story doesn't end here. There are several other things. Ask Bina what happened on her wedding night," said Mini with a sly smile on her face.

Bina was shy. "Why? Why don't you tell your story first?"

Mini said, "The bed was decorated just the way you see in the movies. Strings of flowers hung from the top on all sides. Many rose petals and flowers had been strewn on the bedsheet. Their fragrance filled the room."

Bina said, "The entire room was decorated with flowers on my wedding night too. There were strings of flowers everywhere. Marigold, rose and jasmine buds were all over the bed, emitting an overpowering fragrance. My sister-in-law had arranged my hair beautifully with jasmine buds. I waited for him wearing a Banarasi sari, vermillion in the parting of my hair, kajal, lipstick, and matching ornaments."

"Did you just sit there? Why don't you say what happened after that?" Mini asked.

"Why? Why don't you tell her first? Let Shaku hear you out and then I will narrate my story."

"Don't act coy and waste my time. Lily Bhauja must be cursing me," Shakuntala interjected.

"Come on! You are always in a hurry to run home. Listen to us. It will come in handy for you one of these days."

"Shut up!"

# Chapter 20

Shakuntala was startled out of her reverie when she heard the noise outside.

Had he come? She moved away from the door and stood waiting beside the bed.

No! There was no one!

She looked at the bed. She had heard a lot about it from Bina and Mini. Hers had not been decorated lavishly. But she was not concerned. She believed that the inner self was more important than outward appearance. Nothing else mattered if one's life partner was kind-hearted. Outward decoration lasted only for a day. Every night, every moment became memorable when there was someone beside you who was sympathetic and kind.

She sat and looked at the door, feeling jittery at the slightest sound. She kept looking at herself in the mirror.

She gazed at the dressing table on which a large framed photograph of Amar rested. He was smiling and looking handsome. The picture seemed so lively, as if he was going to ask her something.

She had not been able to see her husband properly since arriving at her new home. Her eyes were now fixed on Amar's photograph.

*Amar!* A shiver ran through her as she pronounced the name. A special niche had been created in her heart for him. It was more beautiful and soft than any bed laden with flowers.

One question kept nagging and scaring her. Why did Amar not want to see her even once before marriage? Savitri Dei had told her that Amar's family had asked for her photograph as he could not get leave to come visit her. But Savitri was not able to send one as Shakuntala had never been photographed. How did Amar agree to marry her without seeing neither her nor her photograph? She wondered if he had agreed only because of his mother. Why should he have wanted to marry her—a girl born and brought up in a village? She had never even seen a town. Besides, what education did she have? Why should an educated and sophisticated man like Amar want her as his wife? An unknown fear overpowered her.

She looked at the clock. It was almost midnight.

Amar had not come yet. There weren't many people at home. There were no friends or relations. Sumi Dei and Chitta Bhai had come but left immediately after the reception. She could not hear anyone talking; they must be asleep. It was lonely. Her parents-in-law were tired, and the less said about her elder sister-in-law the better—she seemed to be working under compulsion. Why wouldn't Amar come? Was he out telling his friends that the marriage had been solemnised against his wishes?

She found no answers. She recalled that her sister-in-law had told her that Amar slept on the roof until midnight. How could he be there tonight? Wasn't he eager to meet her? She debated for a while and then decided to find out for herself.

Just then, the door opened, startling her. She stood up with alacrity.

"Sit down. Why are you standing?" Amar said as he bolted the door.

She kept standing, holding on to the side of the bed.

"Did you see the picture of Lord Jagannath on the wall? Have you paid your respects to Him?" Amar touched the picture and bowed. She arranged her loose hair hurriedly and pulled her sari over her head. She stood beside Amar, bowed to the Lord and then touched Amar's feet.

"Stop! This is not needed; I don't like it."

Amar held her by the shoulders and restrained her. He continued, "Why did you put such beautiful hair into a knot? And you hid them with the sari covering your head. Let your hair down. It looks good on you." He did the needful himself.

Her hair seemed to have turned rapturous all of a sudden when he touched the tresses. They cascaded down her back, the smooth edges reaching her waist.

Amar picked up a string of jasmine flowers from the dressing table and tied them to her hair.

He made her sit on the bed.

She kept her head lowered while Amar just stared at her without saying anything.

She was happy on one count at least. She was sure that Amar would find her beautiful. No one in the village had ever disputed that. Savitri resembled their father, but Shakuntala was completely different. She had a round face, an aquiline nose, and large eyes. She was fair too, exactly like her mother.

She waited for Amar to say something. He did no such thing. She worried again, thinking he would be dreaming of the beautiful girls in the big city where he worked, and therefore why should he fall for a girl like her? He had perhaps married against his will.

"Are you feeling bad because I was somewhat delayed?" he asked after some time.

"No!"

"What were you thinking here all by yourself? You don't know anything about me."

She softly responded, "I was wondering how you agreed to marry me without any knowledge of who I was or what I looked like. I am not sure whether you liked me and really wanted to marry me."

He joked, "Do you think I fancy someone else?"

She did not reply.

"Why are you quiet and sitting with your head bowed? Look straight at me and talk." Amar lifted her chin and continued, "You too knew nothing about me. Yet you agreed to this marriage. Should I also think likewise? You seem to have been pressured into accepting me, haven't you?"

She blurted out, "How does my opinion matter?" adding, "In a way, I had become a burden at home. I was unwanted there. My mother was always bedridden. Father too lost his will and energy when my younger brother married of his own accord. My sister is the only person..." Tears filled her eyes and her voice faltered.

Amar held her palms. The warmth of his touch permeated her body.

"Can a girl as beautiful and gentle as you ever be a burden? Why do you think so? All right! We have married without having known or seen each other. There is nothing wrong with it. We will discover each other's likes and dislikes in due course and fall in love. Now get out of this melancholy mood. I have not seen your beautiful face properly. Besides, you are crying. This is not good."

She tried to stop more tears from falling but failed. Amar embraced her.

It was the first time she had experienced such unrestrained kindness, which brought on more sobbing.

As suddenly as they had flowed, her emotions drained themselves out.

She looked up and saw Amar holding out a glass of water. She gulped it down.

"Mother had told me many things about you but not that you cried for such long periods," he said with a cheeky grin.

Shakuntala just kept looking at him.

"When Mother returned after seeing you for the first time, she praised you to the skies. I fell in love with you right then. Mother never praises anyone unjustifiably and the fact that she did meant you were really praiseworthy."

"You are an educated man used to city life. How did you agree to marry a semi-literate, rustic girl like me when you could have found someone much better?"

"How could I have got such pure gold?"

Shakuntala began to smile.

"Ah! How beautiful you look! A smiling face has its own beauty. I would never have let you cry had I known your smile was so enchanting. Let me tell you something. My heart was filled with love for you from the very moment I touched your hand on the marriage dais."

"But you should have informed your mother about your preferences. Our marriage has to last for a lifetime! Besides, your situation is not as distressing as mine."

"How does it matter? I had never thought of choosing a wife on my own as I believe that the decisions of parents are the best for their children. When my mother chose you, I was sure you must be good. I have got confirmation after meeting you. I could not have made a better choice. My mother has given birth to three sons, and I wanted her to have the satisfaction of choosing at least one daughter-in-law. My elder brother had a love marriage with a classmate without informing anyone at home. With that precedent, my mother never even dreamt that she would be able to select a wife for any of her sons.

"My sister-in-law is a working woman and does not help with the household work. Mother does it all. My sister-in-law will soon deliver. That will mean more work for Mother. She knows it very well and has to tolerate her eldest son and daughter-in-law if the family has to be together. You might wonder why Mother does not employ a domestic help to share the work.

"My younger brother beats up all the servant boys Mother keeps. He forces them to smoke and drink and steal. Finally, Mother is forced to drive them out. It is the same with the girls; no one wants to work here because of him. Thus, Mother has to do everything herself.

"That leaves me. I am a different person. I could not do what my elder brother did. Nor can I be like my younger brother who is a glib talker. I don't earn much and so why would any girl love me? Therefore, it became Mother's responsibility.

"I can very well imagine why my mother selected you. You are exactly the kind of girl she had always wanted as a daughter-in-law. You will take care of everyone at home and she will be spared some of her daily drudgery.

"I have no sisters. If I had one, she would probably have helped her. Mother would have liked you to bring a dowry but she seems to have let go of that desire. I am sure that the girl who won over my mother has to be an extraordinary person."

"Do you think I can live up to Mother's expectations?" asked Shakuntala.

"I am sure. Come, I want to take you somewhere to make this night unforgettable."

She stared at Amar in amazement.

He opened the door slowly and took her to the roof. There were two chairs there. He made her sit on one and occupied the other.

She looked around. The house was a corner one. There were roads on two sides. A car or two passed by at short intervals. A few street lights were burning, but it was dark around the house. A few lights shone in the distance.

In her village, everyone went to bed early and it would be quiet except for a jackal or a dog howling now and then. Shakuntala used to sleep soundly when Savitri was still there. She would sometimes wake her if needed. After the elder sister left for her marital home, Shakuntala would have her mother accompany and talk to her whenever she needed to answer nature's call out in the bushes.

What were they doing on the roof? She had never thought that this night would pass in this way. This was a town, and there were lights far away. She looked up and saw the moon flitting between the clouds. The roof was dark and quiet.

A stray dog barked in the streets. She was startled and clutched Amar tightly.

"Let's go inside. I am scared," she said.

"Why should you feel scared? I am with you. Sit silently for a while. You will come to love the sky, the stars, the moon, this roof, and the darkness. You must be with nature and not see it from afar. You will feel good when you start to understand it. This is my favourite place.

"I sit here until late and talk to all that is up there. I love to chat with them. I have to go back to my room and sleep because I have to go to work in the morning. I don't know if my staying up here like this is good or not, but don't force me to sleep early. Also, don't force me to stay inside the house all the time. I would be happy if you too came up here after finishing your work and sat with me so that we could chat for some time. Do you agree?"

Her palm was still in Amar's.

Chatting with the moon, the stars, and the sky! What strange ideas Amar had! She was afraid of the night and what would happen to her if she sat here until midnight every day. How could she talk to Amar freely when she was so scared?

"You haven't answered me."

"Well, I have to get used to this habit of yours. Do I have an option? You will come here every night anyway. How can I keep waiting for you to return to the room? I will either have to join you or sit alone in the room like I did tonight." She smiled meekly.

"I have been chatting by myself all these days with the cosmos. Now, with you here, I will do so with your hand in mine. Those up there will look down at us and smile." Amar kissed her palm.

Shakuntala made a mental note of the warmth of Amar's first kiss as he moved closer.

"Didn't you wonder why our bed was not bedecked with flowers on a night like this?"

There was a questioning look in her eyes.

"I had forbidden it. I don't like such things."

Shakuntala thought, *I have already preserved this tonight's memories within me.* But she did not say anything.

She still did not reply when he asked, "Do you feel sad that our bed was not decorated?"

He persisted with the question.

"I just never dreamt about my wedding night," Shakuntala finally said.

"What did you dream about?"

She was quiet again. Amar relented and began staring up

at the sky.

Was he feeling bad? Shakuntala wondered if he was upset because she had not answered. So she said, "I feel I was searching for something. I did not know what I was looking for. I understood later that I was searching for love and affection. I never slept in Mother's warm lap. She has been bedridden since the time I was born. She suffered physically. How could she shower love and affection on anyone? I was always in Dei's lap. Father worked hard to make ends meet. I have seen only poverty. The almighty has now fulfilled my desire."

Oh dear! How she was going on talking! What would Amar think?

She looked at him while he stared upwards. He still held her palm. She could feel his grip more tightly now and shut her eyes as a sense of security overtook her.

She opened her eyes when she felt Amar's lips on her forehead.

She did not know when she had fallen asleep, with her head on his shoulder. She was embarrassed. "It's time. Let us go downstairs. You are exhausted. Let us go and sleep," said Amar.

Shakuntala said, "No! It's nothing like that. I was awake for long but have no idea when I dozed off."

Amar whispered in her ear, "It's fine. I will let you go today but there will be no excuses from tomorrow."

They returned to their room. The first thing she saw was the glass of milk. She held it out to Amar. "I should have given it earlier. It has grown cold."

He took something out of his pocket and said, "It's not important. Keep all your ornaments in the cupboard. Somehow, I feel uneasy to see a woman wearing heavy jewellery and ornate saris everyday. I would prefer you wear something light." He sipped the milk. "I have to ask you something. Mother told me that your name is Shakuntala. I have decided to call you Shaku, if you don't mind."

"No, no! Why should I object? I like anything you like. You may call me by any name. I will appear before you as you wish. I do not wear heavy jewellery because I never had any."

"Good! See how our tastes match! There will be no differences if our tastes match completely. There will be no arguments and quarrels. However, our relationship will be sweeter if we quarrel once in a while." He pinched her cheeks and smiled.

"Look at this. Do you like it?"

Amar put a thin gold chain and a pair of small earrings in her palm.

She kept quiet.

"What happened? You didn't say anything. Don't you like them?"

"They are really beautiful."

"Let me put them on you. Wear them always."

He removed the ornaments that Shakuntala had brought and put on what he had bought for her.

She felt ecstatic. She thought that her fasting on Mondays and worshipping Lord Shiva had finally paid off. She had never prayed to Him with any particular aspiration in her mind. He appeared to have showered His blessings on her all the same. She thanked Him and the presiding deity of the village. She also thanked her Dei and Sura Bhai.

Amar held her tightly and kissed her. His love and affection overwhelmed her. She had been neglected all her life. Now she felt valued and appreciated by him. She slept, with her head resting on Amar's broad chest.

# Chapter 21

Amar loved his family a lot. He loved his mother the most. His elder brother, who was an important officer, dominated everyone. He was angry if anyone shirked responsibility. Though Amar's father was alive, the elder brother was the de facto head of the family. His decision was final in every matter. Amar's sister-in-law too had a senior role at work, but Amar himself had not studied much as he was often ill. He had been given his father's job when the old man retired, but it did not pay much. His younger brother, Ajay, gave up studies midway and went into business. However, he got into bad company and spent all his money on liquor. He would not listen to anyone and therefore no one told him anything. He came and went as he pleased, and Shakuntala had never seen him stay the night.

She did all the household work from day one. She toiled the whole day to cook for all. She also took care of Amar's parents and catered for guests and relations who dropped in. Everyone had different preferences, and she tried hard to satisfy them. Soon, they all became completely dependent on her. Meanwhile, her sister-in-law gave birth to a son. Shakuntala not only did the housework but also helped in caring for the child. To add to her workload, Ajay would barge in at any time and, as instructed by her mother-in-law, she attended to him first. All of them were scared of Ajay; Ruli was always near him when he was present. As Shakuntala was used to hard work from childhood, she was not unduly worried.

The only person who made no demands of her was Amar. He did all his work by himself.

One day, she asked him, "Why don't you let me do anything for you?"

"That will be the proverbial last straw which will break the camel's back. As it is, you are doing all the work here. How much more can you do? After all, you too are human! At least let me do what little I can. I help Mother whenever possible."

"Why don't you help me too?" she asked sarcastically.

"You won't let me."

"How do you know that? Actually, you don't want to help me. As a punishment for making a lame excuse, from tomorrow, you will allow me to wash and iron your clothes and select what you wear to the office."

"Your presence is enough for me, Shaku! I did all my work before your arrival."

"I am not going to listen to anything. You have to do as I say."

"All right! How can I disobey you? Your fragrance will be with me throughout the day." He looked at her lovingly, embraced her and kissed her on the cheek.

Usually, Amar munched a few Horlicks biscuits before leaving for office along with his lunch. Since he returned home late in the evening, he would ring her up a few times every day, but she could not talk freely with people around. Besides, she had to complete her work. So, she told him to call only once a day at three in the afternoon.

In the evenings, after the family had eaten together, Amar would go to the roof. Every night, he waited patiently for her to join him after wrapping up her work. He would begin talking as soon as she reached. Shakuntala was learning more about him. She was amazed to see that the man who spoke so little in general could discuss certain topics of keen interest at such great lengths.

She now understood how love and affection could transform someone's life. Amar built a new world around her and she cherished every moment they were together.

# Chapter 22

Shakuntala did not have to cook much dinner that night. Her brother-in-law had taken his wife and some friends for a movie, which was to be followed by dining at a hotel. Ruli wasn't around either; the mother-in-law had gone to visit a neighbour with her grandson. Shakuntala's father-in-law was watching television in the living room. She stood near the window of her bedroom and looked at the gate before going back to bed. Time hung heavy waiting for Amar. She then draped an attractive sari, let her hair down and switched on the fan. Still awaiting Amar's arrival, she fell asleep.

Suddenly, Shakuntala felt someone stroking her head. She awoke with a start and saw Amar in front of her.

"When did you come? Why haven't you turned on the light? Have you had dinner? There was not much to do at home, so I lay down and fell asleep."

"You can sleep whenever you feel like it. Why worry? I just wanted to make sure that you were all right." Amar touched her forehead to see if she had fever.

"Nothing is wrong with me. I was only tired. I'll serve dinner."

"You work like a donkey round the clock. It's only natural that you are tired. You rest. I will serve myself. Tell me what you want to eat and I will bring it here."

"No, I don't feel like eating anything. You eat. Mother will serve you."

"All right! I'll get a glass of milk for you."

She lay down again but could not sleep. She thought that Amar loved her so much that he did not want to even wake her! He must have returned exhausted from the office, but he did not wake her up. He did not even switch on the light. She was grateful.

Amar returned to the bedroom a moment later and asked, "You have been in the house all evening?"

"Yes," she answered briefly. "Why?"

"It's a full moon outside. The entire area is brightly lit. You would have seen it had you stepped out. Drink the milk first."

Amar switched on the light and held out the milk as he gazed at her.

"It will spill," she said and took the glass.

"So you remember?" Amar sat beside her.

He continued, "I thought you had forgotten about today. You didn't say anything this morning or when I rang you in the afternoon. I never imagined you would startle me like this."

"I remembered only when I was waiting for you this evening."

"You dressed specially for me? You are beautiful! Will you do something for me?" Amar asked as he looked longingly at her.

She was amazed. "What?"

"Make your hair into a chignon and put on some lipstick."

She smiled. "I was going through the cupboard today and saw a few saris I had never worn. As I never go out and don't get a chance to wear them, I took one out today."

"Perhaps you don't know, but you have done me a great favour by dressing like this. You surely were lovely at the reception. Today, you look even more beautiful." Amar kissed her on the forehead.

"Drink the milk now. I have one more request," he said.

"You want me to come to the roof with you, no?"

"You guessed it. I would not have asked you if it were not a full-moon night. I want to look at your lovely face in the moonlight."

She stood up even though she was thoroughly tired. She could not resist being with him in the light of the full moon.

Amar led her to the roof. It was bathed in moonlight.

She lay down on the mat that Amar had spread. She closed her eyes while he kissed her forehead, cheeks, eyelids, and lips.

"Can you sit up for a moment?" he asked. "I know you are very tired. All your life, you worked like a donkey wherever you went, and I regret that you have to do the same here."

"I have always worked hard. Why are you worried, and why are you sorry?"

Shakuntala raised her face and continued, "It gives me great pleasure to do something for others. I am happy working here. No one forces me. This is my home, my family. Is not keeping everyone happy my duty?"

"You work for everybody, but they too should think about you! Pratima, my sister-in-law, shirks work, and Mother does not say anything!"

"Change the subject. Shouldn't we talk about ourselves? A year ago, I had neither seen you nor known anything about you. I am very fortunate and pray that you become my life partner in every birth."

Amar gave her a bouquet of red roses that he had brought and slipped a thin ring on her finger. "The sky, the moon, and the stars are witness to everything I do tonight. I left office early. Do you know why?"

He continued, "I was annoyed with you and thought you had forgotten today's importance. I consoled myself believing that you were probably working hard. I bought this small ring and bouquet on the way."

"But I haven't been able to buy anything for you," protested Shakuntala.

"That is because I haven't taken you out anywhere. I promise I will do so every weekend. We will first go to Rourkela and then visit other places."

"It's good that everyone at home has forgotten this day! It doesn't matter anyway. That both of us remembered it is all that matters."

She felt that Amar had become sad and so changed the subject.

"I threw up several times today. Mother was happy, but your sister-in-law was not. 'Why couldn't they delay things a bit?' she asked Mother."

"Why are they behaving like this?" Amar was puzzled.

"You are so knowledgeable. How come you are not able to understand such a simple thing?"

"I really don't understand why she was displeased."

"She said there was a child already at home. It would be inconvenient if another came so soon. They had their first child after five years of marriage. Mother concluded that I am pregnant, but your sister-in-law was unhappy."

"So this is the matter?"

"What do you mean?"

"Do you really want to be a mother? Who will look after the child? It seems you don't love me anymore." Amar rested his head in her lap.

"You won't ask me anything else, and I won't tell you anything more either!" Shakuntala was annoyed.

"Do you have the time to think about our child? You are doing all the work in the house. There is already a child here, and despite its mother, you are more or less its nanny. Are you a human being or a machine? Think about yourself once in a while."

"I know, but I want to present you with a symbol of your love."

"No, no! That has to wait. I cannot load you with more work. We will consider it after a few years."

"I had never imagined that you would fill my lonely life with so much love."

She held onto Amar for a long time while her tears flowed.

She threw up again. Amar made her lie down and gave her some medicines and glucose water several times. He caressed her head. She threw up several more times.

She woke up late the next morning. Amar was sitting beside her. It seemed that he had not slept the whole of the night.

"Oh, no! It's nine already!" Shakuntala panicked.

She continued, "How could I sleep so late? Who is doing the household work? Has anyone cooked? Brother, Pratima Apa and you have to go to work."

"Be careful! Get up slowly. You are ill."

"There's so much work. Aren't you going to office today?"

"No," he said.

"It's all my fault. You stayed awake because of me."

"The human body needs rest. You work hard and haven't eaten anything for twenty-four hours. Besides, you have thrown up several times. So, go off to sleep."

"I'll see what Mother is doing. She must be overburdened."

She tried to get up, but her head was reeling. Amar caught her just as she was about to collapse. She lay down again.

"Sleep and don't fuss. Something is certainly wrong with you. I'll get a doctor. Don't worry about the housework; I will help Mother. She is not annoyed. She came twice to check on you."

Amar went out to call the doctor.

Shakuntala's parents-in-law asked how she was.

Ruli said, "Why are you giddy, and why are you vomiting? Is it good news?"

She did not answer.

Ruli continued, "My son will be happy. The poor fellow never tells us anything. The other two have everyone running around when something goes wrong. Amar is completely different. He never makes any demands and keeps quiet. God moves in His own mysterious ways. He always came first in class. Despite his constant frail health, he graduated and got this job. He was terribly low one day, and I tried my hardest to reassure him. Now he has stopped complaining but lapses into silence. You have made him happy and a child will add to his happiness."

The doctor examined her. He said nothing about the "good news" but prescribed some medicines.

"You cried so much yesterday; it's good you have got rid of all your tears. I do not want to see them in your beautiful eyes again. I didn't say anything yesterday but will be angry if I see you crying again," warned Amar.

"Why didn't you go to office?" Shakuntala asked instead.

"I have decided not to go until you recover fully."

"There's nothing wrong with me. The doctor said I was suffering from acute acidity. I had also hoped like Mother to get some good news. But..."

Amar whispered, "I want a daughter who is as beautiful as you. Quickly, give me a present." He embraced her tightly in his arms and kissed her on her forehead.

She smiled.

The telephone rang.

Ruli said, "Amu! Your office is on the line."

Shakuntala turned on her side and tried to sleep but could not.

Amar returned. "These office people won't leave me alone. I had thought of staying away for a few days, but there is a problem and I have to go. I had brought a key home and now they need it."

He added, "You haven't got up or eaten anything. Take a bath and eat something, and I will be back in a few hours. Don't go out! You might fall and hurt yourself." He caressed her and left.

She stayed in bed for some time before sitting up to eat something as Ruli kept her company. She then did a few chores with her mother-in-law.

"Mother! Please go and sleep beside Pupun. I will do the rest of the work," urged Shakuntala.

She filled the bottles with water and cleared the table, glancing all the while at the clock and the telephone.

She lay down thinking Amar would be angry if he found her working. Sleep evaded her. She drank some water and looked at the clock again. She was worried why he had neither come nor called.

Just then, the telephone rang. She lept and picked it up.

"Are you speaking from Amar Babu's house?"

"Yes."

"I am calling from the office. He felt some pain in his chest a short while ago and has been admitted to the company hospital. We are with him. Please come immediately." The caller hung up.

The receiver fell from her hand as Shakuntala shouted for Mother. Amar's parents rushed to the hospital, leaving her behind as she was not well. She spent the entire waiting period worrying. They finally returned late at night.

"What's wrong with him? Where is he?" The questions flowed out of Shakuntala rapidly.

Ruli was brief. "He is all right. The doctor said that they would keep him under observation for a day or two. Go and sleep now. I am tired and sleepy too."

Worry racked her the whole night.

Five days later, Amar was still in the hospital. His parents went there daily. She asked Ruli several times about Amar, but the only answer she got was, "Why are you so worried? We are taking care of everything. He will come home very soon."

One day, she broke down and told Ruli she wanted to see Amar.

"We will take you one of these days. Why are you worrying so much? He is sleeping most of the time. Visitors are not encouraged. You are crying here and are likely to do so there also. Then the doctors will get angry." She sounded irritated.

"I will see him from afar. I will not cry near him. He has been there for seven days and I am here..."

"Do you also want to be admitted? The doctor said that Amar will be released in a few days. You will nurse him after that. Don't worry so much."

Shakuntala became quiet. Hereon, she did the housework like a robot.

Her anxiety kept her awake at nights. What was wrong with him? He would have certainly telephoned if he were all right.

She felt she was being tortured constantly. She could neither eat nor sleep and prayed every minute to the presiding deity of her village.

She prayed to all the gods and goddesses she knew. She banged her head several times against the wall on which the picture of Lord Jagannath hung.

One evening, Shakuntala went to the roof absentmindedly after dinner and sat at their usual place, with tears streaming down her face. This was the first time the couple had been separated. Who could she share her agony with? The only person who could have supported her was on a hospital bed.

Shakuntala gazed intently at the sky as she questioned the moon and the stars that were so dear to Amar.

"Why have you kept him away from me for so long? Don't you know how difficult it is for me to live without him by my side? Don't you miss him too?"

There were no answers. She entreated them repeatedly. "Make him well again. Bring him back. We will lose ourselves in conversation again."

Her grief was unbearable.

She felt someone's warm lips on the back of her neck and turned around.

The same guileless smile was on his face.

"This is wonderful! You seem to be enjoying yourself," he said and slumped into the nearby chair, taking her palm in his hand.

"Why are you staring at me like that? Are you angry because I went to the hospital without informing you?" He pressed her palm.

She was astonished and could not utter a word.

"It seems you have become quite brave. You are no longer scared to sit here all by yourself. Just see. This sky, this moon, these stars, this roof, this darkness, and this moonlight loved me exclusively. Now they love you more than me. Didn't I tell you that one day they would be your close friends just as they have been mine? How quickly they took to you! I am now jealous of you."

The young woman could not say anything still. Every word she wanted to say was stuck in her throat.

"Why are you silent, Shaku? Say something."

Shakuntala began to sob.

"Come on! Didn't I tell you that I didn't want to see tears in your eyes ever again? I will go away if you cry like this. Don't blame me later."

He freed her hand and got up to leave.

"Stay, Amar! Please stay! Don't be angry. I will never cry again. Don't go away. Please, Amar, don't go..."

Her eyes opened all of a sudden. She looked around. Amar must be thinking about her. Where and how was he? How could she go to him? How could she see him? He had been in the hospital for ten days, and she had not seen him even once. What would he think of her? He loved her a great deal. Was she returning his love like this? Amar had sat by her side throughout the night when she had fever. But she was doing nothing for him when he was in the hospital for so long. She could not put up with it any longer. She would persuade her mother-in-law to take her to him the next morning.

She glanced at Amar's parents' bedroom as she was about to enter her own. The light was still on, and the door was ajar. She wondered why they had not slept until then. She stood near their door.

They were talking with Amar's brothers. Shakuntala wondered if she should go in but decided not to. No one had called her. Perhaps they did not want her to be present. She was about to return to her bedroom when she heard Amar's elder brother speaking loudly. "Don't expect too much from me. Just because the two of us are working does not mean that we have loads of money. We also have a baby to look after. How can we gather enough funds? He has been in the ICU for the past ten days. We have already broken the bank paying for medicines and injections. Hospitals insist on money in advance. He was in the company hospital. You shifted him to a private one. Now, suffer the consequences! I don't have any more money to spare. We don't know if Amar has got any savings. Ask his wife. She should know."

She stopped in her tracks. Was he referring to Amar? She recalled the day when Amar had told her that a friend of his was in the ICU. She had not understood it and Amar had explained that "being in the ICU" meant a patient was in a critical condition. A shiver ran through her. Was Amar in such a bad state? Why had everyone kept her in the dark! She trembled. Her heart beat faster. She found it hard to breathe.

Her father-in-law said, "Don't worry so much. Manage things somehow for the time being. Let him get well. We will find out about his savings later on."

She leaned against the wall for support.

Ruli said, "How much money would he have? He does not earn as much as you do."

"Why not? Why do you think he has no savings? We do earn more but we also spend money on attending meetings and parties and going to different places. He earns less than me but spends virtually nothing. He has also found a wife to match his lifestyle. She is no spendthrift either. She is a simple girl who does not waste money. She wears cotton saris and spends her time in the house. She does not spend money lavishly like your elder daughter-in-law. She does not go to beauty parlours or parties and does not buy new saris and cosmetics every month. My wife often dines at hotels. And then there is the child on whom much money is spent. Amar does not have such expenditure. Ask his wife. They must have saved something."

Amar's elder brother was silent before continuing, "Father! You should find a way out. The doctors said they will have to operate. They will decide on the date only after the money is deposited."

The younger brother, Ajay, said, "I think we should move him to a government hospital. We will get the surgery done there."

Shakuntala's mother-in-law interjected in a supplicating voice, saying, "No, no! Don't say that, son. Private hospitals are expensive, but they take good care of their patients. Besides, government hospitals do not have the advanced instruments that private hospitals have. It is also not prudent to move him from one hospital to another in his present state. The two of you arrange some money. Father will also contribute. Let the surgery be performed first. We will see after that."

Shakuntala could not stand there any longer. She dragged herself to her room. She fell on her bed and wailed. How could she stay at home when Amar was in such danger?

Time ticked away. The pillow was wet with her tears.

With an effort, she got up, wiped her tears and washed her face. Then she opened the cupboard and took out the few ornaments that she had kept there as per Amar's instructions. The thin necklace was the only memory of her mother. There was a pair of earrings, in addition to the four bangles that her Dei had given her and a few rings that had been given to her by relatives. Shakuntala removed from her hands the bangles that Lily had given her. The chain and ring her family had given Amar was also taken out. She tied all of the trinkets in a bundle and waited for the morning.

She carried it to Ruli and placed it before her along with a cup of tea. Tears flowed out of her eyes. She said between sobs, "Mother! I have only this with me. Please sell them for his treatment. Please get him cured, Ma!"

Her mother-in-law stared at her and the bundle.

Shakuntala said, "What will I do with them? Take everything, but please let me see him. You keep saying he will return any day now, but ten days have passed. Neither has he come nor have I seen him. I cannot stay away any longer. I must see him or I will die!"

"Enough is enough! You are unnecessarily scaring everyone. What will you do there? He is in the ICU and no one is allowed in. We sit outside and come home. What will you do there?" Ruli tried to suppress the irritation in her voice.

She continued, "Nothing is wrong with Amar. Patients are kept in the ICU to cure them quicker. He is not very ill. His office admitted him there. There is a lot of work to be done here. Go and finish it. I am already quite worried. Don't make things more difficult. Go and cook. They have to go to the office." Ruli pushed her daughter-in-law into the kitchen.

That day, Sumi made a rare visit. Shakuntala wiped her tears and touched her feet. Ruli took Sumi into her bedroom and Shakuntala noticed that Ruli too was drying her wet eyes as she spoke.

The tears that had dried up for a moment in Shakuntala's eyes began to flow again. She was restless thinking about Amar.

Sumi wanted to go to the hospital to see the young man. Ruli advised her not to. "Wait for a while, Sumi. You cannot see him if you go now. You can meet him only during visiting hours. We will go there in the evening."

Sumi stayed at the house that day.

She lay on Ruli's bed after lunch. As her mother-in-law got ready to go to the hospital, Shakuntala washed the utensils and put the kitchen back in order. But she was agitated all the time. She sobbed at intervals, rushing to the old woman with entreaties.

"Please take me to him today, Mother. I cannot hold myself back anymore."

"I have already said no to you. I have told you that you cannot come. Why are you insisting again and again?"

Shakuntala turned to Sumi and pleaded, "Please request her to take me along. He has been in the hospital for the last ten days. I have to see him at least once."

"Oh! Is it ten days? I was in the village for a month and heard about it only when I returned last night. Why aren't you taking Shakuntala with you, Ruli? How long has she been married? How can she go on without seeing Amar for ten days? Take her once to the hospital. Let her see her husband. She should have been there by his side. I am surprised to see her at home."

Ruli replied, "I am stopping her because either Amar or she could create a scene there, and that would not be good for him."

"It is but natural for her to be upset. How old is she after all? She has been taking things stoically until now. Ruli, let her see Amar. I will ensure she does not break down there. Amar too must be wanting to see her."

"Ask your brother-in-law. I cannot say anything more."

"Don't worry, Ruli. I will deal with him. Shakuntala will be fine after seeing Amar."

"Let her go with her sister-in-law if she has to go. We will go later. I will look after the child while Pratima is away. Call her up and ask her about the visiting hours."

"Bhai will be at home. Can't he look after the child for an hour or so?" asked Sumi.

"It will be difficult for him to manage the child by himself."

Ruli rang Pratima and asked her to take Shakuntala to the hospital.

"Get ready, Shakuntala. Pratima will be returning from the office, and you can go with her. I will stay back with Ruli."

Shakuntala thanked God silently and waited for her sister-in-law to arrive.

Pratima came and took her to the hospital in an autorickshaw.

Shakuntala recalled what Amar had told her some time ago. "You haven't set foot outside for a year. But you will go out now. Winter is in the offing. Both of us will go for walks in the morning and enjoy the experience of walking along the wide roads of Rourkela. We will finish the house work together later."

Pratima told her to control her emotions. "They won't allow you to visit Amar otherwise. Come, we have reached."

The young wife wiped her tears and climbed the hospital steps. Shakuntala's heart was thumping wildly. Pratima was a couple of steps ahead, walking briskly with long strides, but her feet refused to keep pace. The two women ran and entered the lift. It was the first time Shakuntala had done so.

There were people everywhere. Patients were being pushed on wheelchairs and trolleys. Shakuntala followed Pratima mechanically until they reached the ICU.

The guard allowed only one to enter at a time.

Shakuntala was scared.

Pratima had cautioned her to be quiet, especially amid serious patients there, and come out quickly.

Shakuntala was startled when a doctor came out wearing a mask, with a stethoscope around his neck. She was very nervous as she entered the ICU and stood beside Amar's bed.

Many instruments were attached to him. But his face looked like an innocent baby's, complete with a mischievous glint in his eyes.

She touched Amar's feet and saw that he was gesturing with his eyes to come near. The familiar smile was back on his face. With a strenuous effort, he held her palm. His grip was still affectionate but not as strong as before. Tears rolled down the corners of his eyes and his lips quivered.

"Tell me, who is going to talk to me if you keep quiet?" She wiped away his face with the loose end of her sari.

"I have been waiting for you for a long time," he said.

She did not reply but only caressed his head. She knew he wanted to say much more.

Amar's voice trembled. "Control yourself, Shaku. How will you face the world if you are always scared? You must get into the habit of walking by yourself. I know that you can do it and will not stop."

She held back her tears as she asked, "Why are you talking like this? Everyone at home says that you will get well and come back in a few days."

Amar tried to smile.

"You will return, Amar. You certainly will. How can I live without you? Who will teach me? Who will comfort me?"

Amar stared at her, still holding her hand. Her warm tears fell on his chest. She could not suppress them any longer.

A nurse cautioned her, saying, "The patient needs to relax. Go out if you have finished talking, and let him sleep."

She turned her face away and tried to pull back her hand, but Amar kept a steady grip, earnestly staring at her.

"Go now," the nurse said and forced her out.

She heard Amar saying, "Forgive me, Shaku..."

Having returned home with Pratima, Shakuntala still felt the utter silence of the ICU. It was as if she was in an endless vacuum that spread to the sky and breached the boundaries of space.

Soon, Amar left the world for all time to come.

Dei sent Sura to Shakuntala when they heard the news, and he insisted on bringing her to the village for a few days. However, Ruli did not agree. Shakuntala too did not want to go. Amar's memories were in this house, and his fragrance pervaded every nook and cranny. She did not wish to leave the place ever again.

# Chapter 23

Over time, everything returned to normal. Shakuntala did all the work in the house as before. She toiled tirelessly from early morning until midnight, never protesting. No one sympathised with her either. There was only one person who would have shown her some sympathy, but he was no longer in this world. However, she had a gnawing feeling that though she did all the work by herself without complaining, the people in the house were behaving differently. Her mother-in-law would be irritated with her on the slightest pretext and found fault with everything she did. The behaviour of her father-in-law and elder brother-in-law was at times insufferable. She did not know what her mistakes were. Her sister-in-law gave her more work every day. Only the child's behaviour was the same. He still followed her around, yelling, "Aunty! Aunty!"

Shakuntala had begun to say very little. She had also stopped going to the roof and would cry in front of Amar's photograph every night. "Why did you love me so much and then leave me alone? Why didn't you take me with you? Why should I live when you're not around?"

She sat at Amar's study table and looked at the picture of Lord Jagannath. "Why did you give me a husband like Amar if you wanted to do this to me? I was content in my village, ignorant of love and affection. Why did you awaken such sensations within me? How can I live without him now?" She banged her head against the wall and wept constantly.

What amazed her was the behaviour of her younger brother-in-law, Ajay. It had changed completely. He came home every day and had lunch with her mother-in-law quite often. At times, he stayed back at night, too, and chatted with everyone during dinner. He praised Shakuntala's cooking and often asked how she was. He came into the kitchen occasionally and told her not to grieve over Amar all the time. He seemed quite sympathetic towards her.

He once said, "I see everyone is selfish in this house. No one cares about you. All they want from you is work, and they do not bother about your feelings."

Ajay continued, "You are overloaded with it. Why don't you stand up to them? Learn to fight against injustice. Don't be scared. I am with you. It is unfortunate that Amar Bhai died so early. But that does not mean that everyone can take you for granted."

She listened to him patiently but never responded. She had spoken rarely with Ajay in the past, as he was not at home most of the time. But he was now spending more time at home than ever. He participated in all the discussions and expressed his opinions freely. She could not understand what to say to Ajay when he talked like that.

# Chapter 24

Shakuntala hadn't visited the roof for months since Amar's death. Tonight, however, she felt drawn towards it and planned to go up after finishing her chores for the day. She now stared at the sky. The moon had been full days earlier. A few clouds were moving around, and the moon played hide and seek with them. She went to Amar's usual spot and sat down. Tears moistened her eyes.

"Where did you go away? Do you love the moon, stars, and sky more than me? When I asked you so one day, you answered after a long time and only when I insisted. You said, 'What answer can I give to such a childish question, Shaku? My love for them is completely different from my love for you.' However, when I persisted in my query, you just responded with a long, tight embrace. I believe now that you certainly loved them more than me, and that is why you went away to them." Shakuntala sobbed bitterly and covered her mouth with the loose end of her sari to stifle the sound.

She felt someone's warm palm on her shoulders. All she saw was a dim figure.

"Who is it?" There was no response. The shadows parted, and Shakuntala was startled to see Ajay before her. She stood up with a jump.

"What are you doing here at this hour?" she asked.

"Why? I just felt like coming here. Sit down. I wanted to know what you are doing here so late. You hardly talk to anyone at home. Are you talking to Amar Bhai's ghost here?" Ajay lowered himself into Amar's chair and chuckled.

She kept staring at him.

"Why are you still standing?" He pulled her down, onto the chair. "Why do you keep quiet all the time? How long will this continue? Amar Bhai has left us. Will everything stop now? The show must go on."

Shakuntala gazed at the sky instead.

"How does it help to sit here and look for him among the stars? He is already lost among them. You won't get him back whatever you do. Rather, you should look at the person sitting before you." Ajay placed one hand on her shoulder and turned her face towards him with the other.

He continued, "Look at me. I have been waiting to take a good look at you."

"What is this, Ajay? Stay away from me. I don't like this."

She tried to get up but Ajay forced her down.

"Why are you behaving like this? Leave me alone. I have to go downstairs," she insisted.

"I am the only person who can help you. You will regret it if you stay away from me."

She struggled to release herself.

"I, and the others in the house, wonder how a girl who always stayed buried in domestic work could be so clever. You look so simple. Amar Bhai never said anything to anyone! No one for even a moment believes that the quiet and gentle person that he was would be such a lover boy!"

He kept on holding her hand.

"Our late brother is such a great man that he forgot his parents and brothers and remembered only his wife. Who made him a man, and who is going to reap the benefits? The great lover boy! He has bequeathed all his savings to you. This is a classic example of eternal love. Do you know what your dear husband has done?"

She continued to struggle.

"His dear wife is the sole nominee for his bank account and life insurance policies. What magic spell did you cast on him? Hats off to you! Give me a glimpse of that magic." Saying so, Ajay placed his hand around her waist.

At that moment, she hated her brother-in-law with all her heart. She flung his hand away.

"Oh, yes! You will push me away now. Your lover boy has made you rich after his death. We spent our savings on his treatment, and you inherit all his money!" Ajay pushed his face close to Shakuntala's. She thought she would throw up because of the stench of his mouth. She turned her face away in disgust.

Amar had never discussed finances with her. He was a simple and straight-forward person and wanted her to be likewise. She did not need much money for herself. They had never spoken about it.

"The rascal perhaps knew that he was going to die soon and had therefore taken several life insurance policies. Bou is devastated. Being his mother, she had been the original nominee. When did you make him change it?"

Shakuntala said firmly, "I know nothing about this. Amar never discussed it with me."

"Come on! Can anyone believe you? You played your cards well and are now planning to appropriate everything! I don't hold it against you, but stop this farce of crying for him day after day. Listen to me. Let the two of us get together. Then the money that belongs to all will stay within the house and the matter will end."

She got up in anger and nearly stumbled against Ajay. There was firmness in her voice. "Don't talk nonsense! You are taking unwarranted liberties. Don't you ever dare talk to me like this. As far as Amar's money is concerned, you don't have to worry. I will talk it over with your mother." She turned to go downstairs.

Ajay caught her firmly. "Wait! How can you leave like this?" He pulled her towards him.

"Have you ever thought about your current situation in this house? You worked the whole day when he was around, and after his death, you have become a maidservant. You are a daughter-in-law. Why should you be a maidservant? Be my wife, and no one will be able to say anything but treat you as a daughter-in-law once again. Your future will be secure."

She trembled with fear. She had no idea how to counter Ajay's shameless words.

"Are you out of your mind? Aren't you ashamed to talk to your elder sister-in-law in this manner? You changed your behaviour after the death of your brother. And I thought that you had been deeply affected by his premature death. You were sympathetic towards me. I now realise I was completely mistaken. Your brother had told me everything about you. You will never change. You are as depraved as ever."

"You will get to know me when you agree to my proposal. Be my woman and see how things move on from there."

Ajay was in a hurry to force himself on her. He used all his strength to pull her towards him.

"Let go of me, Ajay! Let go! Don't commit such an unpardonable sin." She struggled to push him away. She could not counter Ajay's strength. He jumped on her in a frenzy.

Her blouse ripped open on the side and her sari slid off. Her hands went limp. Whom could she call for help at this hour of the night? Everyone was sleeping. She looked for a way out of that darkness.

Just then, Shakuntala heard someone moving about downstairs. "Ma! Ma!" she shouted as loudly as she could.

Ajay pressed his hand against her mouth to muffle her voice. She fell and Ajay was about to succeed in his endeavour when footsteps were heard coming up the stairs.

Ajay stopped and Shakuntala struggled out of his grasp. She saw her mother-in-law standing in front of her. She slumped down at her feet.

"Ma! I am not responsible for this. She called me here. I never come here so late at night. Ask Bhauja why she had come," Ajay said and hurried away.

Shakuntala's mother-in-law helped her to her bedroom and said, "Bolt the door securely."

The young woman did not come out for a long time in the morning. She sat inside not knowing what to do. She was surprised that no one had come to find out how she was.

After a few hours, Ruli entered her room. "You have got up already? I thought you were sleeping."

"I got up early but did not feel well. I will go now and finish the rest of the work. You must have made breakfast."

"No one has gone to the office today. Don't bother about the cooking. Pratima has finished all the morning chores."

Her father-in-law came in, followed by the elder brother-in-law. The latter had several papers in his hand.

"Sign on the cross marks," he said and spread them on the bed.

Giving her a pen, her father-in-law said, "Sign carefully. Don't make any mistake."

Mustering up some courage, she asked, "What are these papers? Why should I sign them?"

Ruli said softly, "These papers do not concern you. These are the bank and LIC documents. I was the nominee in them, but I don't know when he changed the name in your favour. Therefore, you have to sign."

"But why do you need the signatures now?"

"We will be able to get the money at the earliest this way. The paperwork has already been done by my elder son. If we delay this, it might create problems. Don't ask so many questions. Just sign."

"But why should I sign the bank papers?" she asked again.

Ruli seemed exasperated. "Don't ask so many questions. Finish signing. It's getting late. My son will begin the process. Sign quickly, otherwise he will be angry."

Shakuntala stared at all of them briefly. She then took the pen and signed without a murmur.

She remembered Ajay's words from the previous night. "Amar Bhai has left behind a great deal of money for you. Be mine forever. The money will come to us. Otherwise, they will grab everything," he had said. She now knew what was going to happen but did not have any option but to comply with how things were going.

Her brother-in-law examined each paper minutely before going away. His father followed him.

"A ticket has been booked for you on the night bus. Pack some clothes. Sura will come and take you with him for a few days."

Saying this, Ruli left the room.

Shakuntala now looked at Amar's photograph on the wall.

The next day, Sura arrived to take her home.

Upon reaching her parents' place, she learned more bad news; her mother was no longer alive.

Shakuntala sat down quietly on her mother's bed.

The villagers dropped in to see her. They patted her, embraced her affectionately and cried with her. They were sympathetic.

"The poor unfortunate woman! How she suffered! God was kind to her only briefly. He relieved her of her suffering, but that too did not last long."

Varied thoughts flooded Shakuntala's mind.

*How old would I be now? It seems only yesterday my sister got me married with such difficulty. Did it last? I am back here again. God only knows who will take care of me now.*

*How am I going to spend the rest of my life? My father cannot afford to get me married again, and my brother and sister-in-law are terrible people. They will not allow me to live peacefully. What will I do? I will be a millstone around my sister's neck. There seems to be no one else. My shrew of a sister-in-law won't allow me to stay here. I should have stayed at my in-laws' place. Why did I have to come here? Oh, yes. That's it. Why should I let go of my share of the property? How can I claim it? It would have been better if I had a child.*

Soon, Savitri Dei came and took her back to her place.

Sura said, "Look at the stupid girl! She signed all the papers blindly. Amar had left such a lot of money for her. She gave away everything to those people."

"Let it be. Don't say anything. What could she have done under the circumstances? All right! Let us see what fate has in store for her. Though, it has already ill-treated her by snatching away her husband so early."

# Chapter 25

The days passed uneventfully.

Shakuntala waited in vain for her mother-in-law to call her back. Sura asked Ruli about the matter several times, but there was no definite answer. Eventually, Savitri and Sura gave up trying.

Ruli never called her daughter-in-law back home, and so Shakuntala stayed in Savitri's house. She did all the chores—after all, Savitri and Sura were the only people who were concerned about her.

She worked throughout the day and did not allow her sister to do anything. Savitri only looked after the cattle, goats, and chickens. Visitors suggested to her that Shakuntala marry again. She requested Sura to look out for a suitable boy.

Shakuntala had no time to think about herself. She kept herself immersed in work. Biki, Liki, and Rina—Savitri's children—were extremely fond of her, and she spent her spare time with them. Thus, she tried to forget the catastrophe that had devastated her marital life.

# Chapter 26

One evening, Shakuntala was in the front veranda by herself while the tutor was teaching the children. Dei stepped in and sat beside her.

"Why are you sitting here all alone?" the elder sister asked.

"Just like that."

"Are you thinking about yourself?"

"No, I have stopped doing that."

"Why? You are still young. You want to live alone for the rest of your life?"

"What else can I do?"

"We must do something."

"Why? Am I a burden to you?"

"No, but I am indeed worried. How can you even consider yourself a burden? You are doing all the work and taking care of everything here. But we must find a way forward."

"About what?"

"About your remarriage."

"You want me to marry again? Are you out of your mind? Who will marry me? You should think about your children's future and stop spending any more money on me."

"Don't worry about finances. Think about your remarriage."

"Where will you find me another husband?"

"I don't have to look far."

"How come? Have you found someone?"

"Sura's uncle was here the other day. You have seen him. His son has been lonely after the death of his wife. He has a five-year-old son. I will speak to them if you agree. It will be a simple ceremony with just an exchange of garlands."

"Don't talk about this again, Dei. Have you forgotten that you arranged my marriage and what happened to it? I am destined to be a maidservant, so let me be one in your house. I will not go anywhere. If you need money for my upkeep, I'll work in a few houses in the village. But I will not leave you."

Savitri was upset. "How can you talk like this? Listen to me. Think about your future. Can you stay single all your life?"

"Amar has left, but his love and affection remain. How do you expect me to erase it from my mind? No, Dei. It's not a question of just one lifetime. I cannot forget his love and affection in future births either and will cherish his unconditional love for me. Please don't force me, Dei. I had never thought that a pure-hearted man like Amar would someday come into my life. I am indebted to you and Sura Bhai for it. Though he is not with me today, I cannot commit the sin of marrying again. My body was purified by his touch, and I cannot let anyone defile it now."

Her sister did not say anything more.

# Chapter 27

One day, Dei started feeling dizzy and suddenly fell down. Shakuntala ran, picked her up, and noticed she had a high fever. Sura and she took her to the nearby hospital.

The doctor explained that Savitri's blood pressure was very high. He then advised complete rest and prescribed some medicines.

Shakuntala was certain that her elder sister had been worrying about her and that the resultant stress was upsetting her blood pressure. She was determined to nurse her back to health.

But even sleeping pills were not proving very effective in helping Savitri sleep. When Shakuntala was working, Sura would watch over his wife. But once her domestic chores were done, Shakuntala would massage Savitri's limbs until she went off to sleep, often telling Sura to rest while she cared for the patient.

Savitri felt angry. "Shaku, you do all the housework and then stay awake at night. Who will look after you if you fall ill?"

Shakuntala ignored her and would not leave her unattended. There were times when Savitri could not sleep the whole night and Shakuntala continued stroking her head. She talked about various subjects to divert her sister's mind.

# Chapter 28

A while later, the doctor prescribed stronger sleeping pills for Shakuntala's sister to ease her insomnia. The next day, Savitri fell asleep early after dinner. For the first time in weeks, Shakuntala slept in her own bed. She too drifted into much-needed sleep instantly.

The young woman awoke all of a sudden when she felt a hand moving over her body before resting on her chest. The room was dark and she opened her eyes in a flash.

All she could see were two eyes glowing in the dark as she felt someone's hot breath on her face.

"Sura Bhai...! You...?"

Sura pressed his palm over her mouth.

He whispered, "Don't shout! The children will wake up. Savitri is sleeping well today after four days and is not likely to get up. However, the children are light sleepers and wake up as soon as they hear any sound."

Shakuntala felt around herself, thinking that the children were at her side. There was no one. She was surprised. Where had the children gone? She tried to remember how she had come into the corner room.

"I was sleeping beside the children. How did I reach here?"

"I carried you here with difficulty. Don't shout."

She said, "No, Sura Bhai. Leave me alone. I want to go back to the children."

"Shut up! I told you not to be loud." He pushed her onto the bed and placed his hand on her chest again.

Catching hold of it, she blurted out, "What are you doing?"

"What am I doing? How much longer can I wait? I too have certain needs. You look after your Dei's comforts, but who will take care of me? You have never given me a thought. Haven't I done anything for you?"

She could not hold back Sura's hands. They were frenziedly trying to rip her clothes off.

"You have done a great deal for me, Sura Bhai. Dei could not have helped me at all if you had not supported her. You and Dei are my only support. You are as good as a god for me. I would have been lost without you. My brothers did not help me. You have been more than a brother to me. I am eternally grateful to you. Even God will not forgive me if I do not acknowledge it."

"In that case, you too have some duties towards me."

He brought his face close to hers. She did not know whether to push back his hand or his mouth.

Sura seemed rabid and uncontrollable.

"This is unbecoming of you, Sura Bhai. Please let me go. I admit that I have some obligations towards you. But please do not do this to me. What will Dei say when she hears about it? Should you do this?"

He stopped momentarily.

"Don't you know why your Dei has high blood pressure? I have been trying to explain things to her for a long time. This world is a strange place, and many strange incidents happen. This is not the first time that two sisters are living together with the same man. Besides, we got you married once. What came of it? Your fate is entwined with mine. You finally came to me. Isn't it obvious? How long are you going to suffer like this? You are sensuous!"

He continued, "I told your Dei, 'Why should the poor girl suffer like this while I am around? The body has its own needs and you have turned into a piece of wood. I cannot take it anymore with Shakuntala's beautiful body so near. I pant for her. I will make her happy and she will make me happy. Everything will be fine after that.' But your sister did not listen to me. She was angry and kept on repeating that you were only a child."

Sura now held Shakuntala in a tight embrace with all his strength. She could not get out of it. Sura's muscular arms had become a powerful cage. She was suffocating. Sura Bhai took all kinds of liberties with her while she struggled, cried, and pleaded with him. However, nothing stopped him; he had become a devil.

Her resistance collapsed. Sura was like a ravenous animal that had been hungry for days. He ravaged his sister-in-law to his heart's content. She was utterly devastated.

Although Amar was long gone, his pious love still permeated Shakuntala's body and soul, the memory of his touch othering all sensations in the world outside. But, tonight, Sura had breached this inner sanctum with brute force, decimating its peace and setting it ablaze with rage. Shakuntala wanted to scream her lungs out, rousing the village—nay, the world—from its reckless sleep. But a sudden thought of Dei and her children doused the revolt inside, her fury remaining stuck in her throat.

She had sought refuge in Sura after losing faith in everyone else in the world. She had never, even for a second, thought that a devil lay hidden behind his seemingly godly manner and conduct. Sura Bhai had always been her saviour; today he was a demon.

But Shakuntala felt unable to do anything. She knew that Dei's happy world would crash if she created a scene. She too would lose her only shelter. She did not know what to do and where to go. Who would give her a roof to live under? It was only darkness and gloom ahead. While Sura Bhai ravished her, Dei's innocent eyes blinked before her. She was bewildered and helpless!

# Chapter 29

Savitri recovered from her illness in due course.

However, Sura's animalistic tendencies did not fade. Shakuntala could not protect herself from him in spite of her resistance and entreaties. He played with her numb body for hours every day under the cover of darkness. The corner room had become her bedroom and prison.

"Tell me one thing, Bou," Biki asked his mother at breakfast one day. "Why does Aunty sleep in the corner room and not with us these days?"

Savitri stopped in her tracks. Shakuntala, who was cooking in the kitchen, waited to hear the answer.

"Aunty used to tell us stories at night. We liked her company. Now, she comes to sleep with us at bedtime, but we don't see her when we wake up. She says she likes to sleep in the corner room. Why don't you tell her to stay with us until the morning, Bou?"

"Finish your food and go and study. Don't think about what doesn't concern you. If you do not want to sleep in your room, come to mine. Don't bother about Aunty," Sura butted in before Savitri could say anything.

The children often nagged Shakuntala to sleep beside them. Sura would scold and send them away.

Savitri saw and heard everything but kept quiet. She just brooded and kept losing weight.

One day, Shakuntala noticed a change in herself that frightened her out of her wits. She collapsed into bitter tears.

Sura was unconcerned. "Why are you so disturbed?" he asked. "This is nothing. Abortion is no longer a serious matter, and many are being done every day. I will get you some medicine. Once you swallow a few tablets, you will be as good as new in no time at all. Your sister did this a few times before Biki was born. This is nothing new."

He brought some medicines the next day.

Upon taking the pills, Shakuntala experienced severe cramping and bleeding. The motherhood that every woman looks forward to was now a curse for her. In a matter of a few hours, she lost her first baby.

How painful it was! For years to come, a bone-chilling shiver would run down her spine every time she remembered the cursed day.

Savitri did not mention the subject at all. Shakuntala noticed the dull look in her eyes and sensed her mental turmoil and helplessness.

She herself was eating much less and becoming weaker by the day. But Sura Bhai did not let go of her easily. Despoiling her body had become a habit, and she had no option but to put up with it night after night.

One day, Shakuntala mustered some courage and pleaded with him. "Please leave me be, Sura Bhai. I cannot take it anymore. How long are you going to make me suffer? Think about Dei. What will she think?"

Sura stopped.

She was terribly scared and unsure of what he would do.

Sura did not say anything to Savitri and did not come to Shakuntala after that night. His sister-in-law was somewhat relieved and thought he had finally seen the light. She did the household chores as usual.

"Open the door quickly, Shakuntala," Sura's harsh voice could be heard at the door one night. Shakuntala trembled in fear. It was raining heavily with lightning and thunder. Her limbs were cold. When she opened the door, her brother-in-law rushed into the room and sat on the bed. She stayed glued to the doorway.

"Why are you standing there? Come near." His eyes were blazing.

She remained as she was and wondered if she could run away. Could she save herself from the demon that was Sura?

He jumped up promptly as though he could hear her thoughts and dragged her with his strong hands, bolting the door.

"Don't you see the heavy thunderstorm outside? How can I stay away from you on such a night? I tried not to come but could not restrain myself. Come to me and let us enjoy this rain-drenched night in each other's company!"

"Please try to understand, Sura Bhai. You have had your way with me. Please control yourself now. I can see how Dei is suffering. How much more do you think I can take? Dei knows everything but keeps quiet. She reared me as a daughter. Neither can I die nor can I run away from her."

"Go, try to run away. I will break your bones. You say that your sister is suffering. Why? She is fine, and I am looking after all her needs. I have needs too. Does she bother about them? And why should she suffer because of you? I am not going to someone outside of the house. I am here only. Come to bed, and don't waste time talking nonsense."

Sura would not listen to her entreaties. They fell on deaf ears. He dragged her once again to the bed and satiated his lust like an animal.

Time continued to pass in this manner, and there was no change in the domestic atmosphere except that Dei surrounded herself with a wall of silence.

Shakuntala became pregnant again. The medicines and pain bordered on physical and mental torture. She did not know what to do.

"Take the medicine and get rid of the child quickly," Sura ordered. She did not want to but did so as she was scared of him. The medicines did not work. Sura too was surprised and did not know what to do.

Seeing that worry was Dei's constant companion, Shakuntala realised that mental stress was at the root of her health issues. She did hear Savitri arguing with her husband at times.

"Come with me," Sura told Shakuntala one evening.

She was surprised. Where was he taking her? She looked at her sister, who just sat quietly.

Sura dragged her and pushed her atop his motorbike. She did as she was told.

After speeding through the darkness, Sura stopped in front of a strange house and walked swiftly into it, with Shakuntala following.

There was a man at a table in a stinking room. The young woman felt like vomiting and wondered if he was a doctor.

He told her to sit. He checked her blood pressure, inspected her tongue, and asked her when she had menstruated last.

Shakuntala hesitated to answer but Sura's scolding made her relent. She explained that she was not certain, but that it could have last happened five or six months earlier.

The doctor wanted to know the exact date. When she did not reply, he pointed to a nearby bed and told her to lie on it. She heard him turn to Sura and say, "You have brought her so late. Where were you earlier? Last time, you came at the right moment for the medicine. Why did you delay things now?"

Sura replied, "Last time, there were many outward symptoms, and I noticed them. This time, there were none and she was eating normally."

"It's late now, and her life may be at risk. She will not be able to withstand an abortion."

"Do something. You know everything. Help me out. I won't be able to face anyone if something happens. My three children are growing up. I admit I made a mistake. She seduced me when her sister was not at home. I thought she was lonely, and I only wanted to make her happy."

The doctor smiled, saying, "You have a beautiful sister-in-law, and she is near you all the time. I know your nature. I don't believe that she made any advances. You should have taken the necessary precautions. Everything is available in the market. The rules are strict these days. I will get into trouble if I help you."

"What had to happen has happened. Tell me if anything can be done now. Please try to do something." Sura sounded worried and implored the doctor.

Shakuntala was amazed. How could Sura lie so blatantly? He must have deceived Dei too. What would she think about her? She had done so much for her younger sister, who had destroyed her family life! How could Shakuntala ever meet her eyes again?

Meanwhile, the doctor came up to her and told her to strip from the waist down and open her legs wide. The young woman was deeply embarrassed.

The doctor was staring at her, and she could see the familiar hungry look in his eyes.

"I can examine you only when you lie down. I cannot do anything if you sit."

He pressed her abdomen at several places, and she felt his hands were restless and wandering, just as Sura's had been. She could see what the doctor's hungry looks were hinting at. She put on her clothes as soon as she was allowed to do so. Sura told her to wait outside near the bike.

He came out a few moments later and drove the bike much faster than he had done earlier. She had to hold on to the side handles tightly to avoid falling off.

After that day, Sura became highly cantankerous and would unnecessarily scold her and everyone else at home. He would go out for hours, return late at night, and force her to swallow some new medicines. She wondered why she was living in such misery.

There was no reason to. Why was God punishing her and for how long?

The strange sensation that Shakuntala was feeling within herself led to her developing a great affection for the yet-to-be-born child. She did not take the medicines that Sura brought her and behaved carefully when he was around.

She would often pray to God, asking ardently, "What is your wish? It would have died a long time ago if that was destined, but it is still there and growing."

Despite the external hardships, her pregnancy was a beautiful, magical experience on the inside. She had experienced something similar with Amar, but this was different.

Tongues wagged. Savitri's friends, neighbours and relations, who had earlier praised Shakuntala as a gem of a girl, now hated her. They spoke loudly so that all could hear.

"Look at the elder sister. And look at the younger one. There is a great difference between them. The elder one invited disaster for her family, and the younger one schemed against her for her own benefit. Back at her husband's house, she must have eyed her brothers-in-law and was therefore driven out. She has been here for such a long time. She has destroyed her sister's family. She should have been left to perish. Why did Savitri bring her home?"

"Look at her sister. She has turned into a bag of bones with worry and might die any day."

"The vixen sleeps with her brother-in-law and has an abortion every three months. How do you expect her to remain beautiful? The slut should die!"

Though Shakuntala was agonised on hearing such comments, Dei adopted the silence of the grave. Their father, who used to visit them earlier once in a while, stopped coming altogether.

Lily Bhauja turned up one day. "Did you come here for this reason? You made us believe that you were Sati Savitri personified! You told us that your brother-in-law tried to take liberties with you. Now we understand. It's you who was trying to ensnare him. Would you have left your husband's money and house behind if you were not such a shameless woman? And now you are carrying on with your sister's husband? What kind of a woman are you?"

She continued, "I had the good sense to not let you stay in my house. Your sister loves you so much. Now let her reap the consequences. Father said that he won't even look at you while he is alive. He won't come here either. As for me, I would not even spit on you. How could you be so shameless? How do you go around with such a straight face? If anyone talked about me like this..."

Shakuntala listened to her without uttering a word. Sura continued to be constantly angry with her. He did not allow her to go out anywhere, practically turning her into a prisoner.

She had had no desire to live after Amar's death. But now, strangely, the desire to live was resurging with startling strength. She realised that someone else would also live if she remained alive. She wanted to create a new life despite the hardship she visualised. She wanted to see the living embodiment of her flesh and blood.

Though fear was rising in her, it gave Shakuntala a kind of courage. From childhood, she had been taught to bear everything stoically. She had done so faithfully, but now she wanted to revolt. The child growing within her gave her strength. She made up her mind that she would give birth to it and be a mother.

Shakuntala was unwell one evening and fell asleep. She woke up some time later and saw that it was two in the morning. She was hungry and thirsty. She went to the kitchen for water and heard Savitri and Sura quarrelling. This was an everyday affair now, so she did not pay much heed.

However, when she heard a loud thud, she stopped and wondered whether she should check. Her feet were rooted to the spot. She could hear Savitri sobbing quietly.

Her sister was saying, "Why are you behaving like this? What will make you happy? You have made my life miserable. Why don't you kill me? You will be happy then."

Had Sura pushed her to the floor?

"Why should I kill you? I am going to kill her. The bloody girl is sleeping peacefully with a child growing in her. I am not able to sleep for a moment and am going out of my mind. No! Enough is enough! I must do something."

"What more will you do? Haven't you hurt her enough?"

Sura was quiet.

"Listen to me for God's sake! The poor girl has already suffered much. Don't hurt her anymore. You always think of your happiness. Think about her at least once for a change!" entreated Savitri.

"Girl? Is she a girl any longer? She is so cunning. She cheated me. Look at her nerve! She kept everything hidden from me. My enemy is right in my house and under my nose. She will disgrace me."

"It is you who did everything. How can you hold her responsible? The poor girl has never seen happiness. God snatched everything from her. The demon of a brother-in-law wanted her body, and so she could not stay there. My younger brother's wife did not allow her to stay in our paternal home. Father is handicapped and old. Bou already left us a long time ago."

After a pause, Savitri continued, "I brought the poor girl here because no one allowed her to live in peace. She did all the household work and looked after the children. She became a maidservant. But you couldn't leave her alone. You had your evil eye on her. I tried to get her married somehow, but you prevented me. You took advantage of her when I was ill. How could I protect her? You have behaved depravedly. Her mother-in-law realised she could not save her from Ajay, so she sent her away. She is just a child. She has grown up under your eyes! But you! Curse you!"

"You are cursing me? I will thrash you!"

"Beat me! Who can stop you? Haven't you done it earlier? But I will not hold my tongue. This is the truth! Do you expect me to believe you when you malign her? Not just me, you are telling everyone that she enticed you. Others might believe such lies but not me. Don't I know my sister? She's enduring your slanders just to ensure that her sister's family is not destroyed!"

"Why did you bring her here? You call her a sister? This would not have happened if she had thought of you. And what did you do? Did you listen to me? The two of you are responsible. Everyone is pointing a finger at me."

"Marry her now. Allow her child to be born. Why are you torturing her?"

"What did you say? You want me to marry her? Don't I have any prestige in society? Can I walk on the streets with my head high?"

"Now you think about walking with pride! Why did you not think of it when you satiated your lust by violating the poor girl every night? What happened to your prestige then? What happened to your manliness?"

"Don't talk nonsense. There's no limit to what I might do if I lost control of myself. I will have to cut both of you to size, and I have to do it fast."

"Are you going to kill both the child and the mother?"

"I will do what is needed. And I will do the same to you if you interfere. I will not spare anyone who tries to ruin my reputation. Just wait and see what I will do in a few days."

Shakuntala froze in fear. She returned noiselessly to the corner room and was no longer sleepy.

She was parched. She slumped to the ground and pondered what to do. She could not find a solution.

The next couple of days, Sura behaved mysteriously. She could not guess what he was planning. At night, she shivered with fear and remained wide awake. She did not want to fall asleep, scared that Sura would harm her.

One night, she entered Savitri's room quietly. Her sister was sleeping. The younger son was sleeping beside her and the elder one and daughter were on the floor. Everyone was fast asleep. She looked at Sura's room and saw that it was bolted.

Shakuntala was certain that he had gone out last morning. But had he told Savitri that he was not returning that night? Her sister had not mentioned anything to her. It was already three in the morning. He might not return so late, thought Shakuntala.

She stood on the veranda. She had tried to be close to so many people in her life, but no one had stayed with her. Dei was the only one who had never abandoned her. She was always by her side whatever happened. After going through so much misfortune, she had held on to her sister—including her children, her household, her courtyard…everything—for dear life.What else could she have done? Who was there in her life except Dei? Her elder sister loved her more than anyone else did. Shakuntala was alive today only because of her. Sura had turned out to be a fiend. But Savitri had fought for her at the cost of her own happiness. Sura had often beaten her, but she bore it without complaining. She was now reduced to a living corpse.

Shakuntala looked at Dei. How emaciated she was! She seemed to be completely exhausted.

Even so, she was fast asleep. She was perhaps sleeping peacefully because Sura was not at home. Shakuntala looked at her and the children once again, as though she were taking a mental photo of them, and returned to her room.

She bolted the door, switched on the light and began to pen down her thoughts.

Dear Dei

I do not know what to say to you. No language can express my feelings for you. I can tell you only one thing. I did not receive Bou's love and affection in my childhood even though she was always around. I received those invaluable things only from you. You meant more to me than even my own mother. You made so many sacrifices to see me happy. However, it seems I am not destined to be happy.

I returned to you and became a millstone around your neck. Your family life has been destroyed on my account. Believe me, Dei, I have tried my best to make Sura Bhai see reason. He never listened to me. He has lost his humanity to the devil inside him. I kept quiet for such a long time in deference to you and your family. I put up with all of Sura Bhai's atrocities. What else could I do? I could not see a way out. I cannot do it any longer. The child growing within me has been telling me constantly to not put up with it any longer.

So, we are both leaving. I do not know where I will go. There is darkness ahead of me and darkness behind me too. I have now decided to forge ahead. I might stumble, but I will find my own way.

That's it, Dei. I do not know whether you will forgive me or curse me. I have one request. Please don't try to find me. Oh yes! There is one more request. Your family life is in shambles. Try to set everything right.

Yours sincerely
Shakuntala

She wiped her tears, folded the letter, packed a few clothes in a bag, and stepped out of her room.

Shakuntala looked towards the sky from a window. It was cloudy, but there were a few stars. She went to Dei silently and pushed the letter under her pillow, bowing at her feet.

She then ventured out of the house. The moon was about to hide but its sheen, albeit soft, was still attempting to chase away darkness everywhere. There was no breeze to rustle the leaves. Shakuntala was restless as she knew she had to get to a faraway place where no one knew her before daybreak.

She walked fast, virtually ran. She had been scared of the dark since childhood and had never gone out of the house at night by herself. But now she walked alone without any fear. Her anxiety seemed to have vanished.

She walked at a very brisk pace with long strides. She did not know how many villages she had already passed by.

At daybreak, she found herself at a crossing. She stood there for a while to catch her breath. Looking around herself, she suddenly felt as if a long hand was trying to drag her back to where she had fled from. Shakuntala immediately broke into a cold sweat.

Although she imagined everyone was staring at her, in truth, everyone was going about their way.

Some people gathered beside her. Just then, a bus arrived. The conductor asked, "Are you coming, sister? Yes, Apa, I'm speaking to you." Shakuntala got into it without giving the matter a second thought and sat beside a woman. In a flash, all the familiar faces were left behind. Her village, Dei's house, and everything else. She was travelling on an unknown path to an unknown destination.

"Which stop shall I give you a ticket for, Apa?" the conductor queried.

She looked up to him. What could she say? She was in a quandary.

He asked again, "Where do you want to go? May I have the fare?"

She did not know what to do or say. She responded haltingly, "How far will this bus go?"

"It will go to Hariharpur. Where do you want to go?"

"All right. I'll go there. How much do I pay?"

The conductor looked at her in surprise.

She asked somewhat more confidently, "How much is the fare?"

He did not reply. Shakuntala saw that he and the woman beside her were staring at her.

She put her hand down the neckline of her blouse and pulled out her purse. Taking out a fifty-rupee note, she extended it to him.

He gave her five rupees back and a ticket. The woman beside her was still staring at her strangely. Shakuntala looked out. The fields, trees, and houses were moving as fast as her mind was. The farther she went, the better it would be for her.

"O Lord! Please take me to a place where I will be out of Sura's clutches," she prayed to the presiding deity of her village with folded hands.

A chilly wind hit her in the face. Her hair was in a disarray. She kept the small bag in her lap as she looked out.

# Chapter 30

"Apa! Don't you want to get down? Or will you continue to sleep?"

Shakuntala was confused. She opened her eyes, looked around, and wondered when she had fallen asleep. Everyone had already got out.

"Apa! You have to deboard now. This bus will not go any further. We will stay here for a few hours, collect passengers, and return."

How long could she sit in the bus?

She got off, clutching her bag to her chest. She could feel the sharp eyes of the driver and conductor piercing her back.

Shakuntala soon found herself in a small market. Several people were around. Three roads took off in different directions. She was alone for the first time in her life.

"My dear girl! Why are you standing here? Did you come by the bus?" an elderly man asked.

He asked again, "Are you going to the village?"

She nodded.

"I am also going there."

He walked on, towards the narrow tarred road, and she followed him without hesitating.

"Whom are you visiting in our village? I have never seen you before. Are you going to my village or to the one on the other side of the river?"

She kept quiet.

"It's a long distance. Do you know the way? I think you are coming here for the first time."

"Uncle, I will walk with you. It won't be so difficult." She realised she had to say something.

"Are you visiting somebody?"

"Yes. Something like that."

She kept her responses brief and walked with her head bowed. She did not want to answer questions.

She was terribly thirsty and hungry. Her strength too was waning, and she was falling behind him.

"Dear girl, are you tired?" the old man asked before coming to an abrupt halt.

"No, Uncle. This place is new for me, and therefore, I am lagging behind."

"All right. Try to walk a little faster; there are still two-three kilometres to go."

"Uncle, you walk on. I'll follow."

He did not ask any more questions. He slowed down when he saw that she was not able to keep up with him. A while later, the two reached the embankment.

Suddenly, Shakuntala realised that her companion had not spoken for a long time. She decided that it was the right moment to slip away.

The old man said, "We have reached the entrance to my village. Whose house do you want to go to? I asked you several times along the way, but you did not reply. Tell me now. Or do you want to go to the village beyond the river?"

She looked at him. She had to say something but did not know what. Her throat was dry; besides, she was hungry too.

She said, "I will go to the other village. But I am very thirsty. Take me to your house and give me some water. I will go away after that."

"All right. Come with me. I think you are rather tired after walking such a long distance."

Shakuntala thought he had guessed her predicament by her behaviour. She told herself that she would drink some water first and that rest could come later. The child inside her belly must be suffering.

"Please sit here in the veranda. I will send some water." The old man went inside the house.

Meanwhile, she crashed onto the floor. Stroking her abdomen, she tried to suppress her hunger and thirst. An old lady, possibly the wife of the aged man who had led her this way, stood before her with a glass of water.

Shakuntala gulped it down in one go and asked for more.

She felt better now, but pangs of hunger assailed her still. The child inside her also seemed to be in the same state.

The old woman brought some more water in a jug and poured it into her glass. Her visitor guzzled it up greedily.

"Aunty! I'll wash this glass," Shakuntala promptly said and dashed off to the veranda tap where a soap bar and scrubber were kept.

The old woman observed her keenly as she washed the glass and gave it back.

"Where have you come from? I think you are new here. Are you someone's daughter-in-law here?"

How could Shakuntala respond?

"Why don't you say who you are, where you have come from, and where you will go? You did not say anything when Uncle asked you on the way. Are you deaf or something?" the old woman asked loudly and rather angrily.

Her husband came closer. "You gave her water. Let her go now. Why are you shouting at her?"

He turned to Shakuntala, saying, "Now go your way. Go wherever you want."

"Where can I go, Uncle? I have not come to visit anyone. I don't have a home or anyone to call my own. I am completely alone in such a huge world. I don't have any shelter. I don't have anything to eat. I want to live only for the child in my womb. I will be grateful if you give me shelter. I will do anything you want. I am very good at doing chores around the house. I can do everything."

"Have you done something somewhere? And you have a child in your womb. You seem to be from a good family. Are you unmarried? Have you been driven out of your home for this sin?"

"No, Aunty. Don't say that. This child is my only hope to live. Please give me a place to stay. I have nowhere to go."

Uncle and Aunty looked at each other.

Aunty said softly, "But where do you hail from? What is the name of your village? And there is a child in your womb. We must know all about you if we decide to take you in. The villagers will gossip if I keep you without knowing anything about your circumstances."

"I will tell you everything in good time. I swear to God that I won't conceal anything. Just help me with shelter for now. God has been merciful. He has brought me to good people like you. I do not know what would have happened to me otherwise."

They were silent.

Shakuntala sat on the floor, looking at them. Multiple thoughts were swirling in her mind. What would she do if they did not let her stay? She had liked Uncle at first sight, and now she liked Aunty too. They looked like good people. God was certainly good to her as Uncle was on his way back from his daughter's house in the same bus as her.

She prayed, "O Lord! Please save me. How much pain can you inflict on me? I do not want happiness. Just allow me to survive. Make Aunty listen to my entreaties. You have tied someone else's fate to mine. How can I keep that little being alive?"

She paused for a moment. "Whom am I praying to? Whom am I telling my woes? Has He ever listened to me in the past? I prayed to Him so much during Amar's illness. I banged my head against the walls. Did He listen to me? He took Amar away from me forever. I cannot tell Him anything. He moves in His own mysterious ways. Your will be done, O Lord! Inflict as much pain on me as you wish. I will bear everything."

She looked at the old couple again.

Uncle said, "All right. Stay here for a day while we think it over. Our son is at work. We will discuss the matter with him and then decide."

"Aunty! God will be kind towards you. I don't need anything—just some food to keep body and soul together. Give me some old clothes to wear. I will do anything you say. Let my child live somehow with your munificence." She sobbed the words out.

"It's all right! Don't cry. Come in. Take a bath and eat something first. You seem to be very hungry. Perhaps you haven't eaten anything for a long time. And then there is the child."

Shakuntala bowed at their feet.

She thanked her village deity. "You never heard my prayers until now. Today, for the first time, you have done so. I will pray to you constantly hereon. Who else do I have except you?" She wiped away her tears.

Aunty told her to come in.

Shakuntala now noticed that the house was a large building with several rooms. It was in a village but as good as any city home. A dining table with eight chairs was in the large dining room. Not many people seemed to be around. But there were so many rooms! There was a large room in the courtyard in which were stored bags of grain.

She thought that something was lacking—maintenance, probably. Layers of dust covered everything. Moss enveloped the water tap outside. One slip and someone could fall and get hurt. There were two or three washbasins; they too were cloaked with dust. There was dirt everywhere.

She wanted to begin work immediately and put the house in shipshape order.

Aunty called, "Kuni! Come out and see this girl." Shakuntala stared as the daughter-in-law of the house came out of the kitchen.

Kuni smiled, asking, "What is your name?"

"I am Shakuntala." The words came out haltingly as she bowed and touched her feet.

"Come! I will show you the bathroom. Have a bath and eat something," said Kuni.

Shakuntala's joy knew no bounds when she heard those affectionate words. She followed her mechanically.

"This is the bathroom. The well is on the other side. A few paces ahead is a pond. Bathe wherever you like. Do you have any other clothes, or do you want me to give you some?"

"Not right now. I have some with me."

"All right. Finish your bath."

Abruptly, Kuni asked, "You too are pregnant?"

"Yes."

She smiled.

Shakuntala liked her smile and asked, "What shall I call you?"

"Bhauja. Call me Bhauja. My sister-in-law is older than me. She does not call me Bhauja. I would like you to call me that." The smile lingered on her face.

Aunty's eldest son returned in the evening. Uncle and Aunty did not have to wait for his approval. Shakuntala had bathed, eaten a bowl of water rice, and set to work. The appearance of the house was transformed over the next few days.

Aunty provided her shelter, food, and clothes. Shakuntala had found her salvation. She did not hide anything from her and told her every detail about her life.

Aunty listened patiently, patting her affectionately and saying, "Forget the past. Think about your future. Stay with us. Eat whatever we can provide you and be content. You have suffered enough. Now only think about bringing your child into this world safely."

Aunty had two sons and a daughter. The younger son and his wife and the daughter and her husband lived in the city. Only the elder son and his wife stayed with his parents. He worked in the city near the village and came home on weekends. Therefore, the elder daughter-in-law lived in the village. The others dropped in at various intervals. At times, all of them came together. They spent a few days with their parents. At such times, the house would come alive with great energy.

Bhauja was due for delivery when Shakuntala joined the household. Until her arrival, there was no one else to pitch in with the housework. Aunty had been unable to find a helping hand for her daughter-in-law. Naturally, Bhauja's parents were worried for her health. Shakuntala showed up at the most fortunate hour. Perhaps God had deliberately brought her here. She did all the housework from the moment she arrived. She put Aunty's house in order and made it sparkle to its best potential. She looked after the elderly couple's comforts and took good care of Bhauja. She did not allow her to do any work. Bhauja was in bed most of the time during these days. Visitors were extremely pleased with Shakuntala's work and conduct. She won over everyone with her amiable nature and smiling face.

She practically became a member of the family from day one. Aunty had saved her. Now, she did not have to answer any questions. Aunty answered on her behalf. She no longer feared for her safety and the child's. She had found shelter for both of them by the grace of her village deity. Her child grew safely inside her.

# Chapter 31

The firecrackers bursting nearby startled Shakuntala out of her reverie, pulling her back to the present. She wiped the tears that the remembrance of years past had produced and stood up. The sound of the wedding band music and firecrackers was growing louder. The groom's party was approaching the house fast, which woke up Bharati. She came out and asked, "Bou! Hey Bou! Where are you? Why aren't you sleeping beside me? I am scared. Come and sleep next to me."

"Come, dear. I am here beside you. Why are you scared?"

# Chapter 32

Bharati was adamant. Every day, she insisted on going to school.

Shakuntala promised to send her when she was old enough. That did not satisfy the child.

Finally, one day, Shakuntala decided to buy books, notebooks and a slate for her and teach her at home.

She also bought a *barnabodha*, a book on alphabets, and a few other items. She even bought a bag for them.

Bharati broke into a merry dance. Shakuntala made her sit before the deities along with the books and prayed. She placed a chalk in her hand and asked her to touch the deities. She then told her daughter that they would begin the lessons on Ganesh Puja, but Bharati wanted to dive in immediately.

The little girl kept her bag beside her when she slept that night. Despite her mother's remonstrations, she would not keep it elsewhere.

Shakuntala was happy to see Bharati's passion for studies. However, some unknown fear lurked at the back of her mind. She resolved, nevertheless, to give her daughter a decent education.

She taught Bharati every day. She returned from school, finished the housework quickly, and gave her lessons. First, she drew three circles and introduced the girl to Brahma, Vishnu, and Maheswara. She guided Bharati's hand over them. The child gradually learnt alphabets, numbers, compound letters, words, and sentences.

Shakuntala was amazed to see Bharati's academic prowess. She was extremely intelligent and a quick learner. She had a wonderful memory too.

One day, Bharati held on to the loose end of her sari when she was about to leave for school.

Shakuntala asked, "What are you doing? I am getting late. Don't you see those children in school uniform along with their bags? I have to go."

"I am suggesting the same thing. So many children are going to school, and you teach me at home? When will you send me there?"

"Yes. You will also go. Studying at home is not enough."

"Then why don't you admit me?"

"I'll do it in due course."

"What do you mean by that? It's already late."

"No, no! It's not late. There is still time for you to be enrolled."

"Liku has been going to school for a long time now. All right! He is a little older than I am. But Riku, Niku, Chiku, Tutula, Riki, and Biki are the same age as me. They have been going for a long time. Why are you not sending me?"

"Come on! I have promised that you will also go. Why are you insisting on it at this moment? I will enrol you at the right time."

"You always say this. I have been telling you from the time my friends started going. You always say the time has not come. All my friends are in school. How am I still not ready for it?"

"Don't talk so much. I will meet the village school headmaster soon. You are now old enough. You too will go to school like the others."

"You plan to admit me to the village school? I will never study there!"

"Why not?" Shakuntala was taken aback.

"It is a bad school. It's a cottage with a leaking thatch. In the rainy season, books and notebooks get wet."

"Who told you all this?"

"Riku Bhai, Sania Bhai and Mahia Bhai study there. I have gone to it several times with them and seen things for myself."

"When did you go?"

"You are away at work all day. How can you know anything? At times, I go and sit in the village school."

"Don't the teachers say anything?"

"Occasionally, they ask when you will admit me."

"What do you tell them?"

"I tell them that I am not going to study in such a dilapidated school. Then I run away. Rikuna, Chiku and our own Liku study at the school you work at. It is a good one. It's such a huge building. The children wear shoes and socks. There are many teachers and they are always present. They don't lock up the place and go away like in the village school. The roofs do not leak. Children not only study there but also enjoy themselves. Don't you know all this? They tell me they see you there every day. You must have seen them. Liku told me that the lady teachers sing and dance with them."

"I am getting a headache just listening to you."

"You do not stay at home. How can you know anything? Sania Bhai's mother beat him up the other day because he returned from school with all his books wet. Bhai told me that he had left his books in the classroom and gone out to play.

It rained heavily and the books got wet. What could he have done? I am not going to study in that ramshackle school."

Shakuntala was worried upon hearing this. She had wanted her daughter to study in the village school until Class VII and then shift to another one. Bharati's obstinacy made her think. She was only a child and might not study well if her wishes were not fulfilled. Shakuntala also knew that she would not be able to afford the school at which she worked.

Where to admit her daughter was now bothering her. Bharati repeated the question every night. "Bou! When will I go to school? Which one will I go to? When will my name be enrolled?"

The admissions had begun. She had to finalise something, otherwise a year would be wasted. Bharati would make her life miserable if something was not done soon.

The large school near the *haat*, the daily market, occurred to her suddenly. She had seen many children there and had heard that their results were good. She would go there one day and enquire, Shakuntala decided. Both of them would go there for admission later on.

Shakuntala planned to visit that school the next day. She had to cross the haat school on the way to her own anyway.

She looked at it from outside. A high boundary prevented anyone from seeing the inside clearly. On the board was inked 'NILIMA VIDYA MANDIR. Estd. August 21, 1935'. There was a large gate in the front and three small gates on the sides.

She peeped through one of the small ones. The compound had ample space. The students were standing in rows as they recited prayers, with the teachers in front of them. There was a small garden too. She wondered why she had never seen it earlier and convinced herself that Bharati would be happy there.

She realised she had to talk to the headmaster first. He had to agree to admit Bharati.

"Hello Didi! Are you looking for someone?"

Shakuntala turned around and saw a man in a khaki uniform with a whistle hanging from his neck. "I have been observing you for some time. You have been peeping inside. Do you have any work here? Why didn't you come through the main gate if you have some work?"

Shakuntala moved away.

"I did not know there was such a large school here. I was just curious."

"You should come to the main gate if you want to see it."

"I stood there for some time, but it was closed."

"Do you want to admit someone?"

"Yes. I think I will enrol my daughter here this year."

"It is a wise decision. This is the oldest school in the area. Former students are very well placed. They have become collectors, sahibs, officers, and professors. My father studied here. I studied here, and my son also studies here. His son might very well study here too." The guard smiled.

Shakuntala was happy. She had finally found a school she liked. She would come one of these days and meet the headmaster.

Bharati had already gone through the books that she had bought for her. She did not want to study with her anymore. Shakuntala too could not coach her anymore. She had already taught her all she knew.

Her thoughts were suddenly interrupted. "Do you want to go in?" the guard asked.

"No. I saw the school and stopped. You have spoken favourably about it. I will come with my daughter and see the school properly."

"What's the point of seeing it later? The admission process is going on. Meet the headmaster and enrol your daughter soon if you want her to study here. There are English-medium schools everywhere, but our school is very good. Come with your daughter as soon as possible."

Shakuntala answered with a smile. "Oh, yes. I will come with her at the earliest."

On her way back in the evening, she thought about the school. It was not an ordinary one. It had quite a history and had produced many successful citizens. Her daughter would surely become something if she studied there.

Bharati almost broke into a sob as soon as Shakuntala returned. She asked, "Bou! When will you admit me to school? They were discussing it in Grandmother's house in the neighbourhood, and everyone said that admissions are on. Grandmother asked me when I will be joining."

Shakuntala stared at her.

Her daughter had indeed grown up. She kept tabs on the news.

"Why are you crying over such a silly thing? You will also go to school." Shakuntala lifted her onto her lap.

Bharati's happiness could not be contained. "When will I go?"

"Why are you in such a hurry? Do you think I have forgotten?"

"To which school will I go? You are certainly not thinking about that dilapidated one. I will never study there. Are you thinking about it?" Bharati broke into a loud wail.

She wiped the child's face, saying, "I never said you will study there. You will study at a large school."

"When? At which school? Where is it?"

"The one in the market."

"Are you talking about the school where Liku is studying?" Bharati brightened up visibly.

"No, not that one. There is a much bigger one. You will study there. I saw it today."

"Tell me something about it?"

"Have patience. I will take you there one day, and you can see it for yourself."

"You must take me quickly. I cannot sit at home any longer. You are always busy and don't have time to teach me."

Shakuntala kept quiet.

# Chapter 33

A few days later, Shakuntala went to the chosen school after work. She did not stand near the small gate this time but walked through the main gate.

The guard smiled at her and said, "You asked so many questions that day, but you never came to meet the headmaster."

"Yes. I was not able to come. I will meet him and discuss my daughter's admission now."

"He is not here today. He has gone out for a meeting."

Shakuntala was crestfallen

"What should I do now? Should I go back?"

"Wait for some time. One of the teachers is in charge of the admissions. He can explain everything to you."

The guard went to see if the teacher was available. Shakuntala waited for him to return.

He returned with the teacher.

"Namaste, sir. I want to enrol my daughter at this school. How do I do it?"

"How old is she?"

"She will be six next month."

"Why haven't you enrolled her until now?"

Shakuntala did not reply.

"The headmaster is not here today. Come next week with your daughter and meet him. He will decide. Don't delay anymore. Admissions will close soon."

Shakuntala wished him and turned back.

# Chapter 34

After Aunty finished her puja, Shakuntala placed a cup of tea before her.

Aunty asked, "How come you are still here today? I got delayed for the puja and only just noticed."

"Do you have a holiday today?" she asked further.

"No, Aunty."

"Then why have you not gone? Is Bharati all right? Where is she?"

"Aunty, everything is fine. She is in the other house as she studies in the mornings. She has bathed and is dressed."

"Are you taking her to work today?

"I have taken a leave today, Aunty."

"Why didn't you say so? I wondered how you were still here."

"I am taking Bharati to another school today. That is why I took the leave. I will admit her at the school near the haat."

"Why? Won't she study at our village school?"

"She's not willing to join there. You know how that school is. Bharati has seen it and does not want to study there."

"All right. Enrol her at a good school. The one near the haat is good. The condition of government schools in villages is bad. They are shabby and lack adequate teachers.

The school near the haat is a government one too but very well-run. It is always filled to capacity. I hear that the teaching there is good and that their children do well in the matriculation examination. Take Bharati there. My best wishes for both of you."

Shakuntala felt good upon hearing this. She bowed to her and touched her feet.

When her mother returned, Bharati was studying. She wrote something on the slate and erased it. As soon as the little girl saw Shakuntala, she arranged her books back in order.

"Bou! You said we would go to that new school today. When will we leave?"

"Have you had your bath?" Shakuntala asked, although she knew she had already done so.

"Yes. Can't you see it? Why are you asking me again? You forget everything these days."

"All right. I am serving food." She went to the kitchen.

"Which frock should I wear? You are always in the kitchen. Why don't you finish quickly and change?"

"Come and eat first. Both of us will change after that."

"I am not hungry."

"You haven't eaten anything since morning. How can you go on an empty stomach?"

"Let us go to the school first. I will eat after returning."

"We might be delayed there. You will feel hungry. Come, I'll feed you." Shakuntala sat beside her with chapatis and mixed vegetable curry.

"No. I will eat by myself. You make me eat too much."

"All right. Eat as much as you like."

Shakuntala served herself too and sat beside her daughter.

"Why don't you eat some more? You seem to be in a hurry to go to the school."

"I am not going to eat all this. You always serve too much. I am full."

Bharati washed her hands. Shakuntala realised she was in a hurry to go. She took out a frock from the cupboard and showed it to Bharati and asked, "Will you wear this one?"

"No. Give me the blue one. It will look like a school uniform."

Shakuntala dressed her and combed her hair.

Bharati went to the courtyard with a mirror and examined herself in it. Shakuntala stood behind her and smiled. Bharati no longer liked her to comb her hair.

"Let us go. Why haven't you locked up the house?"

"I am doing it. Go to Aunty and touch everyone's feet there."

Bharati ran to Aunty's house.

Shakuntala placed a water bottle, umbrella, and packet of biscuits in a bag.

The mother-daughter duo set out hand in hand for the school.

On the way, Mani, Bharati's friend, asked, "Where are you going today with your mother?"

"I am going to the market to be enrolled at the school there."

"So you won't study with us at the village school?"

"No. I will study at a big school. How can I study with you in that run-down one?"

Shakuntala noticed that Bharati strutted like a peacock as she replied to her friend.

She admonished her. "You should not talk like that. Her school is important for her, however bad it is. Never talk like that again. You have hurt her feelings."

Bharati did not say anything in reply and started walking faster, holding Shakuntala's hand.

They came to the embankment. Shakuntala walked slowly, something she had never done before. Nari Grandpa's tea shop was the only one at the embankment. People visited it for tea from all over. There was a great demand for the pakodas he made; Uncle often brought some home.

Shakuntala wondered whether in her absent-mindedness she had passed Nari Grandpa's shop. He always enquired about her and her daughter.

"Shakuntala! You are late today. I see your daughter accompanying you. What's happening?"

Nari Grandpa was inside his shop. He was an affectionate person, and Shakuntala liked him.

"Grandpa, I am taking my daughter to admit her to school."

"Where will you admit her?"

"I will study at that big school," Bharati shouted out before Shakuntala could say anything.

"What? Are you going to study at that big school near the haat? All right. Go."

Shakuntala told her to walk faster.

"Bou! How far is it?" Bharati tugged at her hand.

"I have told you it is near the haat."

"How far is the haat?"

"Not very far. The school is there."

"My feet are aching, I cannot walk anymore." Bharati pulled her hand away.

"All right. I'll carry you."

Shakuntala lifted her with difficulty. Bharati had grown heavy. She was almost six now. Her mother had memorised her date of birth.

As they moved on, Shakuntala's hands ached. Her breathing became heavy. Finally, she put Bharati down.

"You have become a big girl, my dear. I am not able to carry you." Shakuntala stopped to catch her breath.

"I did not tell you to carry me. You feed me so much every day that I am gaining weight."

Shakuntala looked at Bharati.

Her daughter was speaking the truth. She had indeed put on weight. Bharati was fair with an oval face just like her mother's. She also had the same thick black hair. Shakuntala recalled Aunty's words, "You said you look like your mother. Your daughter surely looks like you. She will also grow up to be as beautiful a woman as you."

"How long are you going to stand here? Why did you force me to eat so much that I have become fat?"

"Let us go. You talk too much. How can you study if you do not eat properly?"

Bharati said again that she was tired. Shakuntala knew the child had already walked a long distance. The young woman was used to walking long distances from home to school and back every day, but it was difficult for a child. Bharati's feet must be aching but what could she do?

"You are my darling daughter. Just walk a little more. We will soon reach the school."

Tears welled up in Bharati's eyes. She said, "No! I cannot walk any further."

Shakuntala did not know what to do. Autorickshaws were readily available around the school but not in the village. Had she known that the distance would be too much for Bharati, she would have asked Aunty to find someone who could drop her at the school on a cycle.

Bharati continued to stand there. Tuna came up just then. He asked, "What's the matter? Why are both of you standing here?"

Tuna lived near their village and sold fish in the market.

Shakuntala had met him at Aunty's house and bought fish from him several times hence. He was on a cycle.

"Tuna! Where are you going? Where is your fish basket?"

"I haven't taken any fish to the village today. I have to deliver some for a wedding party and will sell the rest in the market. But why are you standing here?"

"I am taking my daughter to the school near the haat. She walked up to here but is tired now. Her feet are aching. I don't know what to do. I wonder how she will travel the remaining way."

"I will carry her on my cycle. She can sit in my shop until you come and collect her."

"That would be nice. She won't have to walk anymore. Will you go on Tuna Bhai's cycle, my dear?"

"No! I won't."

"Why won't you come with me? You can sit in the shop and wait for your mother to arrive. She can walk faster if she is alone," Tuna interjected.

"No! I won't go with you."

"What's the matter, my child? You say you are too tired to walk anymore. You could easily reach the haat if you go with Tuna."

"I told you I will not."

"But why? You say your feet are aching and that you cannot walk anymore, yet you refuse to go with him. Why? Go, my dear. Don't be obstinate. He has his work and is being delayed because of you," said Shakuntala, adding, "Take her, Tuna. She will go with you."

"No! I will not go with him. My frock will become dirty if I sit on his cycle. Also, I will smell of fish."

Shakuntala was amazed at Bharati's reasoning. She had never thought of it.

"How your daughter talks! Children today are so intelligent. All right! You walk. I am going." He sped away.

Shakuntala said, "Let's go. You have rested enough."

They began walking again. "Bou! How big is that school?"

"It's pretty big with a high boundary wall around it."

"How high?"

"So high that you cannot see anything from outside. Neither can you see out from inside."

"Are there many children?"

"Yes."

"Have you seen the school before? Why didn't you enrol me earlier?"

"I did not know about it."

"Then how did you come to know of it?"

"I was looking for a good school after you rejected the village school and the idea struck me. Then I came to see it."

"Are there many rooms in it?"

"There must be. It is such a big school."

"Is there a big playground?"

"There must be one."

"Haven't you seen it?"

"No, I haven't. I had gone there only once to talk about you. Earlier, I had seen children singing the prayer in a large open space. You will know everything when you join. You can tell me everything when you return from school."

"Bou! What will the teacher ask me?"

"Let us reach there first. We will see."

"Will I be admitted even if I cannot answer the teacher?"

"Why can't you answer? You remember so many things. You can answer every question."

Shakuntala walked ahead as she answered her daughter's queries.

# Chapter 35

"Bou! I am thirsty." Bharati stopped again. Shakuntala gave her some water from the water bottle. "How much farther? I am hungry too. I cannot walk anymore."

"I have brought some biscuits for you. Eat a few and drink some more water. You won't feel hungry anymore."

"I don't want biscuits."

"Then what do you want?"

"Give me something else."

"I don't have anything else! I knew this would happen. That's why I asked you to eat properly at home. But you did not listen. You ate only half a chapati."

"Buy some chocolates for me."

"All right. You can eat them on the way. By the time you finish, you will be at the school."

Shakuntala took Bharati to a paan shop along the way and bought four small chocolates.

She gave Bharati one and put the other three in her bag. "Why don't you eat one?" Bharati asked.

"No! I have kept them for you. You can ask for another after this one." They began walking again.

An autorickshaw full of children passed them. Shakuntala pulled Bharati closer to her while the child looked at it.

"Bou! Will I go to school every day like that?"

"Yes."

"It will be real fun. Have you already bought books, notebooks, a school bag, and the uniform for me?"

"Let your admission be done first. I will buy them later."

"Buy a pencil box also."

"All right."

"I don't want an ordinary one. Buy me one like Liku's."

"All right."

"Bou! Is there water in the school, or do I carry it from home?"

"We will find out."

"Did you study in such a large school? Where was it? Why haven't you ever shown it to me?"

"Don't talk so much. You will tire yourself out."

Bharati became quiet. She ate up the chocolates one after another.

"Give me some water, Bou. And tell me now where the school is. We have been walking for such a long time, and I still cannot see it."

"I told you that it is just before mine. Have you forgotten?"

"Then we still have to go a long way. I cannot walk anymore. I have hurt my foot." A few tears ran down Bharati's cheeks.

Shakuntala could not carry her. The poor child was in pain. She should have made better arrangements. She blamed herself. Shakuntala looked around. They could be late. It would be inconvenient if the headmaster was away somewhere like the other day. She would have to take another leave at work. She was worried.

"I cannot walk any further," Bharati cried out loudly.

"Come on. Why are you crying?"

Shakuntala wiped Bharati's face. How could she console her? She didn't want her daughter to walk any further, but was there an alternative?

She tried to reason with Bharati. "You are my darling daughter. Just be brave. We will take an autorickshaw once we reach the road. We will be there soon."

Bharati understood and didn't complain anymore. She held Shakuntala's hand and dragged herself after her.

An autorickshaw came and stopped near them. Shakuntala was startled. She had seen Babuni ferrying children to her school every day.

"Didi! Where are you going with your daughter? Haven't you gone to work today?"

"Where are you going at this time, Babuni? How come your rickshaw is empty? Aren't you carrying the children today?"

"I told them I would not be able to take them today. My autorickshaw needs repairs, and I am going to the garage."

"Are you going towards the market or somewhere else?"

"My brother-in-law has a garage near the market. I get my vehicle repaired there only. Why is your daughter so sad? Where are you going, Didi?"

"We have a problem. Please drop us near the market. She is too tired to walk anymore. She has hurt herself and is finding it difficult to walk. Thank God you have come at the right time."

"Climb in. Where shall I take you?"

"Take us to the large school near the haat. I will be admitted there today," Bharati said happily as she sat in the autorickshaw.

Shakuntala said, "God has helped us today."

"Bou! Will I come to school every day in Babuni Bhai's autorickshaw?"

"Let us get you admitted first. We will think about other things later. Sit quietly for a while. You have been chattering away. Don't talk too much, otherwise your head will ache. Then, you will not be able to answer the headmaster's questions."

"I can answer any question he asks. You must be having a headache. You sit quietly."

# Chapter 36

Shakuntala leaned back in the auto, closed her eyes, and drifted into the past...

"Remember one thing, Shaku. We have to ensure one thing about our child. We must see that he or she studies a lot. Our fates were similar. You were very good and wanted to study but could not because of your family's poverty. I too was a good student and wanted to study but I could not as I was ill most of the time and therefore had to give up my studies. This should not happen to our child. He or she must have the desire to study. Even if I do not have anything to eat, I will see to it that our child is highly educated and becomes a high-ranking officer. He won't be a clerk like me. You will be on cloud nine as the mother of an important officer."

Shakuntala listened to Amar silently.

"Why don't you say something, Shaku? Did I say something wrong?"

"No, you are not wrong, but wait till we have a child first. You are always delaying it."

Amar had smiled. "We will have a child soon. I am delaying it because I fear you will love it more than me. We won't delay it anymore, but you must assure me that you will love me more than you love it."

"No! I will love it more than you."

"What did you say?" Shakuntala ran away as Amar tried to grab her.

# Chapter 37

"Didi, we have reached."

Shakuntala opened her eyes and looked at Bharati. She had fallen asleep. The poor girl was thoroughly exhausted.

"Bharati! Get up! See! We have reached your school."

Bharati woke up with a jerk.

Shakuntala sprinkled some water on her face and arranged her hair.

"How much should I pay, Babuni?"

"Finish your work first. I will take the money later. How will you go back?"

"I haven't thought about it. I don't know how long I will be here."

"The garage is nearby. Call me when you are through. I will take you back if my work is done by then."

"All right."

Bharati was awestruck. "Bou! What a big school!" Her face lit up visibly.

The school looked bigger to Shakuntala than what she remembered. She was happy that Bharati would study here.

Some children were going in, and others were coming out.

The children were also buying eatables from the many vendors there. Bharati gazed longingly at the ice creams but turned her face away immediately.

The same guard was at the gate. He smiled at her.

"So you have come with your daughter, Didi?"

"Why is there such a crowd outside the gate? Classes must be going on."

"The morning shift is over, and the day shift will start. Since there are many students, the school works in two shifts. The young children come in the morning, and the older ones later in the day."

"Is the headmaster present?"

"Yes. But you cannot meet him now. It's time for the morning prayer. You will have to wait for a while."

Shakuntala and Bharati stood at one side.

The children stood in rows and sang the prayer.

Shakuntala was happy. She remembered her own schooldays when she used to sing the same one.

Recalling those days, she could still see her headmaster with his paan-stained teeth delivering a moral lesson. Shakuntala used to be the class monitor and would stand beside the teachers.

Bharati shook her back to the present, exclaiming, "Bou! Let us go in."

"Wait some more. We will go after the prayer is over."

The teachers in the school where Shakuntala worked also related important events of the world after the prayer. She looked at Bharati, who would soon be listening to the news regularly. She would recount everything in the evening. Shakuntala had already decided to make Bharati a teacher.

"Bou! Why do you keep ruffling my hair?" Bharati moved away and tried to arrange it herself. However, it looked even more disorderly.

"You have spoilt it. Let me rearrange it," said Shakuntala.

"No, no. I'll do it myself."

The guard said, "Didi, you can go in now. Meet the headmaster first as he will be busy later on."

"Can we go straight to him?"

"Yes, I will tell his peon. He will take you to him."

The school was an old three-storeyed building. The verandas were long, and the classrooms opened out to them. The students had already taken their places. The classrooms were named after Madhusudan, Gopabandhu and the like.

Shakuntala and Bharati followed the peon.

There were flowerpots on both sides of the verandas. The place was neat and clean. Shakuntala liked the ambience.

She stopped in front of small garlanded images of Gandhi and Gopabandhu.

"Bharati, who are these people? Pay your respects to them."

"This is Gandhiji, and the other one is Gopabandhu. You told me about them the other day," Bharati said as she folded her hands.

Shakuntala reminded Bharati to greet the headmaster as soon as they entered.

Bharati replied impatiently, "I remember it."

The headmaster's room had a picture of the Jagannath Trinity on the wall. There were flowers in front of it and incense sticks were smouldering, spreading their fragrance in the room.

She prayed to them, "O Lords! Please help my daughter."

The headmaster was sitting behind a large table, wearing white trousers and a blue shirt. He wore thick horn-rimmed spectacles.

"Please sit down." He signalled to a chair.

Shakuntala bowed to him and sat down.

There was a thick sheet of glass on the table with several papers under it. Bharati also paid her respects to him and kept standing.

"Dear child! Sit on this chair."

"Do you see the clock?" the headmaster asked Shakuntala. "Why is it behind me?"

Shakuntala could not answer.

"I have a watch on my wrist and a small clock on the table. Why then is there a clock behind me? That is for those who sit in front of me to know the time. You have been sitting here for long without saying anything. Time is passing. Tell me why you have come."

"I want to enrol my daughter in your school, sir. I work in the nearby English-medium school. My daughter has a great desire to study at a good school. I had come earlier too but was not able to meet you. Will you allow her to study here?" Shakuntala said it all in one breath.

He glanced at Bharati, who was looking around the room, and asked, "Will you study at our school?"

Bharati nodded.

"Nodding won't do. Say yes or no."

"Yes."

"What is your name?"

"Bharati."

"What is your full name?"

"That is also Bharati."

The headmaster looked at Shakuntala, who lowered her face.

"You were looking at that large photograph. Whose is it?"

"Pratibha Patil."

"Who is she?"

"She is the first woman President of our country."

"What is the name of our country?"

"India."

"What is the name of our state?"

"Odisha."

"Which is the biggest river of Odisha?"

"Mahanadi."

"Name the capital of our state."

"Bhubaneswar."

"What is the name of the Father of the Nation?"

"Mahatma Gandhi."

"Who was the first woman Prime Minister of our country?"

"Indira Gandhi."

The headmaster gave her a slate and chalk and told her to write a few alphabets as he dictated them.

Bharati wrote them.

"Have you learnt to write compound words? Can you write as I dictate? Do you know the story about the thirsty crow drinking water from the pot?"

The headmaster asked her several similar questions.

Bharati answered all of them.

Shakuntala was amazed at seeing Bharati's confidence and the ease with which she answered.

"Who has taught her all this?"

"I have taught her, sir. She is keen to study and has a wonderful memory. She remembers everything I tell her," said Shakuntala.

The headmaster asked Bharati, "Do you know the multiplication tables?"

"Yes."

"How many tables do you know?"

Bharati was quiet.

"Can you write the table of five?"

"Yes."

"Wipe the slate clean and write the table on it."

Bharati began writing.

The headmaster asked Shakuntala, "How old is she?"

"She will be six next month."

"All right. We will enrol her in Class I. Fill in this form. Fill all the columns correctly. Don't make any mistake in the name of the child, her parents' names, and her address."

Shakuntala examined it. She was not sure how to fill certain columns. She sat there with her head bowed.

The headmaster asked, "What's the matter? Can't you write?"

Shakuntala merely looked at him.

"All right. Give it to me. I will fill it for you."

Shakuntala heaved a sigh of relief. Her handwriting was bad. She was also not certain that she would be able to write correctly.

"What is the name of the child?"

"Bharati Priyadarshini."

"Just Bharati Priyadarshini?"

"Yes."

"Date of birth?"

"9 February 2011."

"Mother's name?"

"Shakuntala."

"Father's name?"

Shakuntala did not answer.

"Tell me the name of the father."

Shakuntala was still silent.

She thought that her world was collapsing. She had never imagined that she would have to answer such a question for her daughter's admission. Bharati had never wanted to know who her father was. She had to face this question today and that too in front of her!

"Father's name?"

What answer could she give? What name could she mention? The man who was instrumental in her creation never wanted to be her father. This child never existed for him. It was only a symbol of his lust. He had wanted her to be aborted. He had tried his best to achieve his objective. He had even planned to kill both the mother and the unborn child.

She was too scared to relive those memories.

Why should she associate the name of such a man with her daughter's? How could he be her father when he had never discharged the responsibilities? The girl had never seen his face. She did not know him and would probably never know him.

He was the devil incarnate. He did not want to be known as the girl's father as he thought his image would be tarnished. Why should her daughter carry the baggage of such a demonic name all her life? She was a child of God. Her name could not be associated with the name of a devil.

It was the woman who always endured the suffering, thought Shakuntala. It was she who carried the result of a man's lust in her womb for nine months. It was indeed strange that people wanted the name of a sinner to give an identity to a child! He may not be willing to be known as the child's father, but his name was necessary to establish the child's identity. It was a strange society. And how illogical were its rules! Why had they been made?

Let no one answer her questions, Shakuntala resolved. She did not understand anything. All she knew was that she was Bharati's mother and that her existence proved Bharati's identity. She did not need any other name for it.

The headmaster said, "Your daughter has written the tables very well. I asked her to write the table of five. She has written up to ten without a mistake."

Shakuntala stared at him.

"Oh, yes! I asked you the name of the girl's father. Why did you not reply? Tell me his name."

Shakuntala continued to stare at him. He seemed to have many more questions.

The headmaster rang for the peon. He entered and asked, "Sir, do you need something?"

"Bharati, my dear. Go around our school with Sanjay. This is a big school. There are many trees. There is a lovely playground on one side. Go with Sanjay Bhai. Sanjay! Show her everything. Come only when I send for you. Go with him, Bharati!"

The little girl looked at Shakuntala for reassurance and went with the peon.

The headmaster said, "All right! Tell me now. What is the name of the girl's father?"

Shakuntala sat with her head bowed.

"Why do you become quiet when I ask you this question? Tell me if there is any difficulty. I may find a solution. Nothing will be achieved if you sit quietly like this. I have a great deal of other work. I cannot afford to spend so much time on just one child. You have been here for a long time. Many people are waiting for me outside.

He continued, "Tell me quickly. What is the name of your daughter's father? How can your daughter's name be enrolled at our school without the father's name? You can tell me if you have any problems. I sent Bharati away because I suspected you were embarrassed to speak in her presence. Tell me now and be quick about it."

Shakuntala continued to sit with her head lowered.

"I can do no more for you. If you do not say anything, it is your choice. But I cannot spare any more time for you. I gave you so much time because your daughter is an intelligent child. I like her, and she will do well in studies. I am sure of it. I wanted the child to study here, and so I waited for your answer for such a long time. But you remain silent. All right. Don't say anything if you don't want to. Take your daughter away and come when you are prepared to say something about the girl's father. Remember! The name of the child's father is essential if you want to have her admitted here. You may go."

The headmaster gave his final ruling.

Shakuntala heard everything.

What could she tell him? What could she do? He had already told her to leave. He had said that the name of the child's father was essential for admission. The name had to be written on the form. Otherwise, Bharati could not study here.

Bharati's tearful face appeared before her.

She could hear her voice, "Bou! Am I not going to be enrolled here? Am I not going to study in school like the other children? I want to go to school. I want to study, Bou!"

No! She could not allow this to happen.

Shakuntala made up her mind. There was no point in going back. This matter had to be settled once and for all.

The headmaster stood up and said, "All right! Go now! I have to leave too. I have a meeting."

"No, sir. What I was trying to say..." The words came out haltingly.

"Do you want to say something?"

Shakuntala swallowed hard before saying, "Please write Shakuntala in the column where the girl's father's name is required."

"I am asking you the name of the child's father. You have already told me that the mother's name is Shakuntala. Why are you repeating it?" The headmaster was exasperated.

"Yes, sir. That is what I am saying. Shakuntala is also the name of Bharati's father."

The headmaster was now thoroughly irritated. He said, "Why are you repeating the mother's name again and again? Does your child have a father or not? What is his name? Your daughter cannot be enrolled here without it."

"Yes! My daughter has a father. But I am not going to write his name on the form as Bharati's father. The reason is that she does not need the identity of her father. He was a man who did not know how to respect his own blood. I don't want my daughter to be known by the name of such a person. How can my daughter accept him as her father when she has never seen him? I admit that a child needs a mother and a father and that its identity reflects both of them. But a man turned Bharati's mother into a commodity of pleasure alone. And Bharati is the result of his lust, which is undesirable. That man forced himself on a woman and considered it a stigma to accept Bharati as his child. Society and prestige were more important for him. Fatherhood was secondary.

"Therefore, my daughter, Bharati, has only one identity. She is my daughter—the daughter of her mother! She is Shakuntala's daughter! I am her father and her mother. The only identity that she has is that she is her mother's daughter. She is Shakuntala's daughter and nothing else. My daughter is not going to be identified in society by her father's name. She will never lose her way because of that identity. I will not allow it to happen. My daughter will live in this world with the identity I give her and will walk confidently with her head high. She will study and become someone important one day.

She will create her own identity. She will be known by her own identity. She will show a new path to society."

Shakuntala was breathless. She drank the water on the table in one big gulp.

The headmaster sat with his head lowered. Several thoughts crossed his mind. What kind of situation was this? He had never faced anything like this in his life. No one had ever sat before him and told him about such an identity.

He looked at the table calendar before him. It was just one month to his retirement. He was in a dilemma. He had worked as a teacher for such a long time and was now at the fag end of his career. He had admitted so many children in his long career, but no one had ever put him in such a spot. The identities of the mother and the father had merged to become one. There was a demand for a new identity before him. He was going to retire in a month, and this was a major test for him. It was his job as a teacher to examine students and award marks. But today, he was being tested. A critical question loomed large before him. He had to provide an answer.

He looked up at Shakuntala.

She was looking at him with hope and apprehension both writ large on her face.

"Shakuntala, I have understood what you said. I have nothing more to ask. Your arguments are strong and sound. But there is still one thing that needs attention. There are two columns in the admission form. Two different names need to be written there. They have to be of two different people. One of them is the name of the child's mother. The other is for the child's father. Your form is also the same. I need two names. Your name is one and you are not prepared to divulge the other.

"What can I do? I am bound by the rules. How can I disregard them? I have to abide by them. I accept that your child is fit to be admitted here. She has answered all my questions correctly. On the other hand, you too have provided sound arguments about her identity. But the father's identity is needed as per rules. Tell me what I can do."

She stared at him while he repeated, "Tell me what I can do."

"What can I say, sir? I have said all that I had to say. It is up to you now."

"What decision can I take? There is nothing I can do about it."

"What is going to happen now, sir?"

"What else? Your daughter cannot be enrolled here."

Shakuntala sat quietly.

"Does that mean that I have to go, sir?"

"Yes. I cannot help you."

He started going through the files on his table.

Shakuntala stood up and picked up her daughter's school bag.

"I am going, sir. Namaste."

The headmaster did not look up. He just said, "Namaste."

Shakuntala moved towards the door.

"Bou! Are you leaving already? Have I been admitted?" Bharati ran and embraced her.

What answer could she give?

"Bou, you know something? The school is indeed very large as you said. Sanjay Bhai took me to the playground. It is huge. There are mango, jackfruit and wood-apple trees and flower plants. Sanjay Bhai took me to Class I. Many pictures had been drawn on the walls. Even you cannot identify many of them. This is indeed a good school, Bou. I will study here. You always wanted me to study and become an important person. I will fulfil all your wishes if I study at this school.

"Why don't you say something? What did Headmaster sir say? I have answered all his questions correctly just the way you taught me. Will I be enrolled here or not?" Bharati shook Shakuntala.

The headmaster looked at Bharati and said loudly, "Who says you will not be admitted here? You are a wonderful girl. You will be enrolled today itself. You will study here, I assure you.

"Shakuntala! Take the form. I have filled it in. You just need to sign it."

Shakuntala was astonished at what she had just heard. The headmaster's words took her breath away.

"Why are you staring at me like that? Take this form and sign it."

He said, "Times are changing. The environment is changing. The situation is changing. Social attitudes are also changing. Then why do the rules and regulations made by society not change? It is true we have to abide by them. But human beings are always beset with circumstances that cannot be ignored. We have to face them squarely. Therefore, rules and regulations need to be changed. Such changes are welcome.

"You are right, Shakuntala. Of course, it took me some time to absorb what you said. But I understand everything fully now. I could not immediately grasp it as no one has ever told me such a thing in the past. No one ever told me that a child could have such an identity. You have opened my eyes. Someone cannot be called a father if he does not respect his own blood. Why should your daughter be known as his? Your daughter should be known only by your identity."

Shakuntala signed the application form and gave it back. She came out beaming with pride and satisfaction.

She could see hundreds of children like Bharati before her. She could see the faces of their mothers next to them. Someone murmured that Bharati was Shakuntala's daughter! Indeed, she was the daughter of Shakuntala and that was that.

# Acknowledgements

I am indebted to Ms Namita Gokhale for showing faith in my writing and for putting me in touch with the team at Om Books International, who have brought this fresh translation to fruition with the utmost care and love.

My heartfelt thanks to my editor, Ms Soumya Duggal, for her painstaking editing and sagacious feedback. A debt of gratitude to Mr Shantanu Ray Chaudhuri, editor-in-chief, for steering the project with his characteristic expertise and Mr Ajay Mago, publisher, whose support was invaluable, especially with regards to conceptualising the cover. I'd also like to acknowledge the efforts of my dear friend Himansu Sekhar Khatua and the cover designer, Mohammad Arif.

My sincere thanks are also owed to Dr Dipty Patnaik for her masterful translation. Finally, my brother, Dr Achyuta Samanta, has been a lifelong cheerleader for my literary pursuits, for which my deep appreciation will never cease.